The House on

Beale Street

The House on Beale Street
A Riley Press Publication
P.O. Box 202
Eagle, MI 48822
rileypress@yahoo.com

Cover by Colleen Nye

Editing by Genevieve Scholl
Formatting by Colleen Nye

Copyright © 2018 Loraine Hudson
Printed in the United States of America

This is a work of fiction. All characters and situations appearing in this work are fictitious. Any resemblance to real persons, living or dead, or personal situations is purely coincidental.

Chapter One

Starting over means different things to different people. For some, it's giving up; for some, it's escape from a painful reality; for some, it's a necessary evil. For me, it meant none of those things.

I simply wanted to do something different, and I couldn't have been happier as I stared down at the kitchen utensils arrayed on my new oak table, in my new kitchen, in my new home. A four-place setting of silverware, a spatula, a paring knife, a potato peeler and a garlic press. Perhaps that last item wasn't strictly necessary, but a woman has her preferences. Mine? Fresh pressed garlic. The garlic press had to stay. I also had four water glasses, four wine glasses, four heavy Blue Willow coffee mugs, a set of Blue Willow dinner plates, salad bowls, breakfast bowls and bread plates, plus a platter— again, perhaps not absolutely necessary, yet since starting over was all about me, and since I had a soft spot for Blue Willow, the Blue Willow platter had to stay, too.

Everything fit so nicely in my freshly-painted cupboards with the cup hooks and the light blue, scented paper on the shelves. Just enough china for me and Natalie, and a guest or two. Just right.

When I made my announcement, "I'm moving to a tiny house in Burtonville," I got a variety of reactions.

"What are you running from?" asked my friend, Louise, who has an MFA and studies and writes tragic poetry.

"Well, hell, Marianne," said my friend, Duffy, who has wanted—ever since my husband, Duane, was killed in Afghanistan—to be more than a friend.

"Awesome!" said my stepdaughter, Natalie. "You'll have a bed for me, though, right? Even in a tiny house?"

I answered them, respectively:

"I'm not running from anything, Louise," and,

"Honestly, Duffy, it's not like I'm moving to Mars. I'll only be thirty miles away," and,

"Of course! I'll always have a place for you, Natalie, my dear."

I found my dream house on quiet Beale Street in Burtonville, a community of about three thousand people. To be fair, it wasn't a true tiny house, which the Internet classifies as sized between 100 and 400 square feet. I had a whopping 657 square feet of living space for me and my dog, Rowdy, who wasn't actually rowdy, but who weighed 140 pounds and was inclined to drool. Though only a tiny bit—a completely acceptable amount in my opinion. I also had a porch, a two-car garage and a large basement where I would one day store things like my Christmas wreath and a bin of Natalie's crayon drawings that I couldn't bear to part with; that is, after I got all the previous owners' things out. Tackling the basement was not a project to which I looked forward.

Back to happier things. For Rowdy, a yard with an invisible fence and a huge oak tree that cast rippling shade across the grass and almost out to the cornfield beyond my property line.

One might ask why I chose to leave the place I had shared with my beloved husband, and where we raised his daughter. Why I would sell nearly everything I owned, the Blue Willow excluded. The answer was simple. Because I wanted to.

I decided the day I looked at myself in the mirror—at my salt and pepper hair in its curly, layered cut; at my brown eyes and my still-smooth skin—and contemplated the energy that I could feel radiating out of me, physically and mentally. As I conducted my assessment, I asked myself what I wanted to do that day. I love to do things—anything, everything—but to my surprise, I couldn't come up with an idea that interested me.

I looked around at the home Duane and I had renovated and decorated with such joy. I gazed at Duane's photo of the Grand Canyon that hung over the couch, at my pottery vases, at the coved ceiling and the hardwood floor we installed ourselves, and I realized I wanted something different. I wanted to make a new place from scratch—make it whimsical, make it sassy, make it beautiful, make it all mine. That I could indulge myself with the rather impulsive act of taking on a new home was due to Duane's forward-thinking, and his insistence on a large life insurance policy. That, and my surviving spousal benefits from the military. Duane gave me the gift of independence.

So, I pursued my wish. The house in Burtonville was definitely all mine, and would be even more so when I finished its facelift. It was in ragged shape— displaying everything from peeling paint, to piles of debris, to crumbling drywall—having been unoccupied for the better part of a year. I approached my new home brandishing paint cans and sanders, drills and saws, and was confident it would be perfect when I was finished. A perfect place for me to put my feet up and sip a glass of wine late in the evening. A perfect place for me to decorate and re-decorate to my heart's content. A perfect place to be peaceful or to find adventure, whichever happened to make its way down the tranquil street where I would make my home. A garage for my Prius so I didn't have to clean off snow and frost in the winter, and what more could a woman want? Perhaps a tree branch strung across the big picture window with a row of artificial birds. Yes, another perfect. I made a note to check the craft store next time I visited Louise or met Duffy for dinner in Peoria.

Meanwhile, I had a cup of decaf on my back porch with Rowdy camped out on my feet, a piece of paper and a pen on my lap, in case I had another brainstorm like that branch-with-the-birds idea, and a view of the cornfield that seemed to go forever on and on in to the distance. Rowdy and I in a tiny house nestled in a small town, with the world ahead of us ... I sighed a selfish, satisfied sigh.

I was contemplating the notion of hanging a wallpaper border with knights on horseback in the room I would use as my den when there was a knock on the front door. Climbing over a loudly-snoring Rowdy, I left the porch and navigated the cluttered living room, avoiding tools and two large sheets of drywall, then opened the door to a smiling woman with her hair in a long, blonde braid. She was wearing red jeans and a T-shirt that shouted *Bonjour*! and she carried a tray of chocolate chip cookies.

"Hello!" The woman balanced the cookies in her left hand and held out her right. "I'm Ashley Midden from next door."

"Marianne Reed." I clasped her hand in a warm shake, and backed inside, relieving her of the cookies when she thrust them in my direction. "Come in! I wish I could offer you somewhere to sit,"

I added, refusing to be embarrassed by the general disarray. "I'm renovating and … well, you know."

"Oh, no problem," said Ashley airily. She perched on the edge of a sawhorse and glanced around the room. "Can't quite tell what-all you're doing here, but I'm sure it'll be nice. I'm so glad someone bought this place. It was getting to be quite an eyesore. Not," Ashley went on hurriedly, "that it isn't a real nice house. It's just that it's been vacant for a long time, and no one bothered to take care of it or even mow. And the people who lived here before, an older couple—you knew that, right—?" I opened my mouth to answer, but Ashley chattered on. "Well, they couldn't really keep up with things. It was high time their kids stepped in. They're living in Pennsylvania now. Oh! That's a pretty color."

I glanced over my shoulder at the rolls of lavender wallpaper I had stacked in the corner.

"Is that for in here?" Ashley strolled over and touched one of the rolls. "Such a pretty color," she repeated. "Like a sunrise. Like right before the sun shows, you know?"

And just when I was wondering how I could politely get rid of her and get back to work, I began liking her. "Yes," I said. "Exactly that shade. It's why I picked it. May I offer you some—er—I think I have some tea around here. I was drinking coffee. It's decaf. And instant," I added. "Coffeemaker's in one of the boxes."

"That would be lovely. Instant's fine." Ashley leaned back on her sawhorse chaise, and I went to the kitchen to fetch coffee and put the cookies on a plate.

"The yard looks way better already!" called Ashley. "Who planted all those chrysanthemums for you?"

"My friend, Duffy," I called back, trying hard not to remember the disapproval on his face when he saw my beloved new home. We'd had a spat about that.

I didn't completely blame him. The house *was* in poor condition, but I was pretty sure what was really bothering him was that I'd moved to begin with. He'd hoped for years that perhaps we might take our friendship to a new level. But I'd held back and I wasn't really sure why. He was caring, gentle, devoted to me—and good looking, too. Tall with straight, sandy hair and pretty hazel eyes. When he was prescribed glasses, he didn't want to wear them until I told him how really distinguished they made him look. It was a sweet memory.

After the first argument, things had settled down and I thought we were okay until that last day—right after the movers had delivered my cartons—when something happened that set him off and he left, coldly and abruptly. He hadn't called in four days, and that wasn't like him. I'd finished cleaning out the last of my things in the old house in

7

Peoria and locked the door behind me without even saying goodbye to him.

"The flowers are real pretty." Ashley smiled when I walked back into the living room with two cups of coffee and her cookies on one of my Blue Willow plates. "I always think yellow shows up the best."

"Me too," I answered. "Which house is yours?"

Ashley pointed down the street. "Just over there. I would've come by earlier, but it seemed as if you were not at home or busy moving, and there was someone here one day. I didn't want to intrude."

I frowned. "Who—?" I began, but Ashley was pointing at Natalie's photograph perched atop one of my dusty end tables.

"Do you have kids?"

"Yes, a daughter. She's away at college." I leaned back against another sawhorse, looking around for somewhere to set my coffee cup and failing to find anywhere flat. I finally put the cookies on top of a pile of paint cans and balanced the cup against my thigh.

"Oh." Ashley's face fell. "My son's a junior in high school, and I'm dreading him leaving when he graduates. He's looking at schools in California."

"It's tough," I said. "You get used to it, though. Natalie's planning a visit in the next few weeks—" I broke off at Ashley's sudden look of alarm and swiveled around to look over my shoulder. It was only Rowdy strolling in from the porch, although he did look a bit like a black bear. Or perhaps a bit more than a bit.

"I didn't know you had a dog." Ashley rose slowly to her feet and backed behind the sawhorse.

"Oh, yes," I answered. "He's—well—rather lazy and quiet. You probably didn't notice him." I hoped Rowdy wouldn't start drooling.

Ashley didn't move. "Lazy and quiet?"

Rowdy ambled up to me and set his chin on my lap. I moved the cookies out of reach. "Lazy and quiet," I affirmed. "He's been here all along. You just never heard him. Usually he's sacked out on the porch or under the tree in the back yard."

As if to demonstrate the truth of my words, he groaned and flopped down next to me, propping his jaw on my foot. I gave my lap a surreptitious wipe. Only one small spot of drool. Not bad. Ashley edged around the front of the sawhorse again and, keeping one eye on Rowdy, she resumed her perch.

"What's his name?"

"Rowdy," I answered, staring down at his prone body, at the gentle rise and fall of his big rib cage.

"Rowdy? Really?" Ashley gave me a quizzical look and appeared to be quashing a smile. "What breed is he?"

I raised an eyebrow. "Hmm, I'm not sure. There's probably some Newfoundland in there. Maybe some Rottie? You know, Rottweiler?" I shrugged. "He came from the animal shelter in Peoria. They begged me to take him during their big black dog promotion."

"Big black dog promotion?"

"They're hard to adopt out."

"Oh," said Ashley, then, "He's kind of cute. He's just rather large."

"Large and in charge." I grinned, deciding Ashley and I were going to be friends. "Or large, anyway."

Ashley took a sip of her coffee and giggled when Rowdy emitted a rumbling snore. "Sacked out. I see what you mean."

I nodded, and she settled back against her sawhorse.

"So how much time do you have?" she asked suddenly. "I need to catch you up on every little thing!"

"Um, every little thing?" I asked.

"*Every* little thing. And how much coffee have you got?"

Chapter Two

Two hours later, I'd discovered that Ashley knew practically all there was to know about Burtonville ("I grew up here, you know!") and along with that, practically all there was to know about the residents.

I found out that the Burtons—yes, related to the original founding family—had marital issues and their sons had joined the Marines to get out of the house. I found out the high school was overcrowded and Ashley's son, Joe, hated his English teacher. I found out that the neighbors on the west side of my house, the Paulsens, didn't like dogs and I should keep Rowdy away from them because if his 'defecations'—I thought Ashley's word was charming—were as large as he was, then he wouldn't be popular there. I assured her I would keep him at home. She said the community used to consist mainly of retired couples, but as people died or moved away, a lot of 'city-citizens'—another

Ashley-ism—came to live in the suburbs like Burtonville. The schools needed funding to accommodate all the new students, yet it was nice that a lot of the old houses were getting fixed up. I learned that the pastor of the local Methodist church had a rummage sale every other month and there were lots of good deals to be had. I learned that the best place to buy fresh produce was at Leonard's—also the best pizza around—and that, although the druggist's wife had died years ago, he still talked about her as if he would find her at home with dinner on the table when he closed up for the night. I discovered that a family on the next block had seven children and a house not much larger than mine, and their kids tended to wander from home to home looking for somewhere to be—or maybe seeking a little space. And I learned that Ashley liked to talk. Liked to talk a lot.

Finally, she took a breath and glanced at her watch. "Look at the time! I've got broccoli soup in the slow cooker, and Joe—that's my son—will be home soon. I better get a move on."

"It's been fun." I stood up and tried to shake the soreness out of my legs where I'd been balanced on the sawhorse for such a long time. It *had* been fun, although my ears felt as if they were beginning to droop, we'd polished off most of my instant coffee sipping and getting refills, and the chocolate chip cookies were a thing of the past.

"Oh!" Ashley exclaimed. "We ate every single one of those cookies! I better come over and bring you some more. I can't believe I ate so many. I just love to visit!" I smiled as Ashley brushed cookie crumbs off her jeans. "Darn it," she added. "I wish we had more time. I wanted to hear what you thought about the robbery!"

"What robbery?"

But Ashley had managed to steer around the construction debris to the front door and had her hand on the door knob.

"Ashley, wait!" I laughed, following her. "What robbery?"

"You don't know about it?" She looked shocked, and at the expression on her face, I didn't feel quite so much like laughing anymore.

"No, I don't," I said. "What robbery? If I come help you get your dinner on, will you take another few minutes and tell me?"

She looked at her watch again. "Deal." She walked back to sit down against her sawhorse.

I looked doubtfully at mine, and resolved to call and ask for an earlier delivery date for my living room couch and chairs, even if the renovations weren't done. The back of my legs felt as if they were permanently dented from my temporary seat. I climbed over Rowdy, who hadn't moved a millimeter from where he'd been since he came in from the porch, and tried to prop one leg over the edge of the two-by-four that constituted my sawhorse chair.

"So," began Ashley, "Mrs. Abbott ... she lived in that big house two streets over and two houses down. The one with the gables and lace curtains. You know it?"

I shook my head.

"Well, she had this giant estate sale—or at least that's what she called it, even though she wasn't dead. Don't you think that's odd? Maybe you don't actually have to be dead to have an estate sale." Ashley stared out the window for a moment, her brow wrinkled.

"Anyway ..." I prompted.

"Anyway," she echoed, and went back to the tale. "She had this big sale, and she had all these paintings she'd collected, rooms full of them, of flowers and bridges and churches and fields and mountains and stuff. It was a good collection, and I know a bunch of city-citizens were here buying them, and even a gallery at somewhere-or-another out west. The sale went on for several days, and she sold a lot of her paintings. I'm surprised you haven't heard this story. You sure you haven't? Olivia Abbott?"

I shook my head. "Nope, sorry."

"Huh." Ashley shrugged.

"And?" I was afraid we'd run out of time before she ever made her way to the end of the story.

"And," said Ashley, "the sale went on and on, and then some guys walked in there pretending to

14

be buyers, but, in fact, they were robbers. And—can you believe it? —there was an off-duty cop from Prairie City who just happened to be there. The cop spied them stealing and called them out. One of the men took off across the yard and through the field behind your house, with the cop chasing after him and calling for back-up. For a while, the guy—the robber, that is—disappeared, and they thought he was hiding in the corn."

"What happened to the other robber?" I asked.

"Drove away. Left his buddy behind in the cornfield."

"Did they catch him? The one hiding in the corn?"

"Nope. Well, sort of. He was gone for hours. Then he popped out and made a run for it down your driveway and into Beale Street. He had a phone up to his ear and he wasn't watching where he was going, I guess, because a car—actually, it was Madeline Burton driving—mowed him right down. She always drives too fast, but maybe that day it was just as well, because she squashed the robber flat as can be."

My stomach gave a little lurch. "Squashed him?"

Ashley grimaced. "Yup. The car must have hit him straight on, because she killed him."

"Right here?" I exclaimed. "In front of my house?" I looked out the window. It seemed hard to imagine a quiet little town like Burtonville could ever be the scene of a robbery and a chase like that, let alone a—um—squashing.

"Right here," said Ashley. She stood up, looking at her watch again. "You don't have to come over and help," she added. "I've got plenty of time to get the table set. How about coming another time instead and we can talk some more?"

I nodded. "Okay, a raincheck, then."

I made a mental note to dig out my coffeemaker from the pile of boxes in what would soon be my office and Natalie's room, and to buy some good coffee and some croissants for when I went over. It was nice to have met one of my new neighbors from the village. I looked forward to meeting more of them. I climbed over Rowdy again, drawing a smile from Ashley, and walked back to the door with her, held it open and let her out ahead of me.

In the driveway, she turned around. "Back to the robbery thing," she said. "I always thought—and a few other people did, too—that maybe the robber hid in your basement while they were searching for him. You can get to your yard from the cornfield, and your basement's got an outside door."

My stomach lurched again, but for a different reason. "My basement?" I repeated weakly, and Ashley nodded.

"I can tell you more later, although that's most of the story."

"Okay." I wondered if I wanted to hear more. The idea of someone hiding in my basement while they were making a getaway from a crime scene wasn't comforting. I gave myself a little mental poke. *Don't be an ass. The guy's dead.*

Ashley waved and walked down the driveway toward the sidewalk. "Hey, Ashley," I called, and she stopped. "Did the paintings get squashed, too?" *What a tragedy for an elderly woman with a prized collection*, I thought.

"That's another thing ..." Ashley began. She started to turn and walk back, then pulled her cell phone out of her pocket. "This is Joe calling."

I flapped my hand at her. "Let's talk later." She nodded and left.

I gave myself a little shake. Robbery or no robbery, it was time to get serious about the drywall. I moved a few things around, pulled the sawhorses out of the way, and found my bucket of drywall mud under a drop cloth. A few minutes later, I was happily smoothing putty over the seam tape and humming to myself. I'd work an hour and then go get a pizza from Leonard's. I got two panels completed, and was preparing to plop a big blob of mud on the next seam when the word "squashing" shoved its way in to my head and I hurriedly set down my putty knife. Duane always accused me of having a dubious stomach, and Ashley's graphic description of the demise of the local thief had definitely put a crimp in my plans for dinner, no matter how much I tried to cheer myself up with the idea of a carry-out pizza.

Besides, something else had occurred to me. I scraped the mud off the putty knife, sealed the bucket of drywall mud and wiped my hands on a rag. "C'mon, Rowdy!" I called to my still-snoring dog, and when he didn't move, I bent over him and said, "Rowdy! You lazy bum!" in one ear. That comment made him open one indignant eye, and he raised his big head. I gave him a push. "C'mon outside with me, buddy."

I could see him considering that. Finally he heaved himself to his feet, shook loudly and thoroughly, and ambled to the back door, following me out to the yard. He sauntered off—perhaps to take care of some defecations—while I went over to the door that led to my basement. I paused in front of the wooden barrier and frowned, then reached out and tried the handle. It turned easily in my hand—just as it had when I'd inspected the house some weeks earlier—and with a squeak it swung inward. The familiar musty smell greeted my nostrils. When the former occupants moved out, they'd left piles of stuff that needed to be disposed of—tools, magazines, blankets, old furniture, boxes of who-knew-what, but no key to the door. I'd left the basement as a Do That Later project, choosing to focus on the upstairs first.

I remembered my realtor, Loretta Jackson, commenting during the inspection, "I'll get a lock on that door. You don't need anyone coming in here and stealing all the copper pipes. Even in small towns like this one, you can't be too careful."

And I remembered seeing the new hasp and a padlock before I moved in—Loretta was nothing if not thorough. So where had the lock gone?

Chapter Three

I resolved to call Loretta the next day and ask her about the lock. In the meantime, I had other projects to focus on; namely, my living room. Leaving the drywall mud to cure, I spent a pleasant hour organizing and straightening, digging my wallpapering tools out of a box, and making a shopping list for the home improvement store. Then I unpacked one of the cartons I had stuffed in the den and sorted through post-it notes, binder clips, highlighters and flash drives, all jumbled in a tangled mess. Why hadn't I spent a little more time trying to organize my packed items? I'd ignored the problem of unpacking—mostly, I just wanted stuff out of the old house.

I carried a box of miscellaneous office clutter I didn't need into the bedroom and set it with the other things I'd decided to throw away or donate. I wanted to make room for my computer on the little desk in the room I would use as my office when Natalie wasn't visiting. Which reminded me that I needed to call and find out when the cable company was going to make an appearance. I cared nothing for television, but I wanted my Internet connection up and running. I added that to the To Do list.

Wondering about the missing lock caused me to forget—almost—the squashing and I decided I did want dinner after all, so I pried Rowdy up from his spot on the porch and he and I ambled down to Leonard's, where we ordered a pizza to go with mushrooms and extra cheese, and a hamburger for Rowdy.

We carried our treasures back to the house on Beale Street, and I settled down at my kitchen table, my pizza in front of me and a beer in my hand, Rowdy at my feet slurping his burger. Outside, the crickets began their evening serenade, and there was a light breeze blowing in the window, bringing the scent of someone barbecuing and the sound of several children shouting and laughing. It was soothing, quiet, small town noise, and I felt content and fulfilled. Mostly content and fulfilled.

I couldn't help fretting about Duffy. I wanted to call him, but something held me back—something that wanted him to call me instead. After all, what had I done wrong? I had told him of my plans for the move, and he knew I was getting restless in the big house Duane and I had shared. After his initial hurt, it seemed as if we were on the right track. He had been helping me by sweeping out the garage and breaking down boxes for recycling, and then he'd planted all those chrysanthemums in my new garden. Why had he suddenly stormed off and then gone so silent? I didn't get it, and I felt alternately hurt and angry. Surely, I didn't deserve that.

I carried the last slice of pizza into the living room and stared at the plastic bin of photos sitting by the rolls of wallpaper. The box contained snaps of Duane and me—some from before we were married, some after—a zillion of Natalie, and even some of Duane's first wife, Iris, Natalie's mother who had died so tragically young. On a sudden impulse, I walked into the kitchen, set my plate on the counter, snagged my cell phone and dialed my stepdaughter's number.

"Mummy!" came her eager voice, the greeting that never failed to make me smile.

She adopted that endearment early in our relationship, after she'd committed some small infraction and had begged me not to tell Duane. "Mum's the word," I assured her, and I'd been 'Mummy' from then on. She didn't remember her biological mother—she was an infant when Iris died—but she was seven when Duane and I married. One of my fears at the time was that I wouldn't be accepted into their little twosome. A pointless worry, as it turned out. Natalie had opened her generous arms and welcomed me instantly.

"What'cha doin'?" I asked her.

"Homework, what else? How 'bout you?"

"Eatin' pizza. Listening to life in a small town."

Natalie giggled. "Thanks for the pictures you sent. Can't wait to come see what you've been up to."

"Well, don't expect too terribly much. At the moment, I think things are worse than when I moved in. I'm making progress, though. It's a lot of tearing down before building up, you know?"

"Are you having fun?"

"Oh, yeah." I told her about Ashley's visit, about my idea for the branch across the window, and the knights-on-horseback wallpaper border in the den/spare bedroom.

"Ooh! Knights!" said Natalie instantly. "I love it! But keep the cat pictures from my old room for the wall. I still need those!"

I grinned. "Okay."

"What's this Ashley like?" Natalie asked.

I hesitated. "Well, if you want to know anything concerning anyone in Burtonville, she prob'ly can tell you. She's got a son in high school, and I don't think she works outside the home. To tell you the truth, I didn't learn a whole lot about her; more about the town. I may ask her to go to Peoria with me to the craft store."

"For your bird project?"

"That and other things. Oh, yes. She told me about some excitement here."

"Excitement? In Burtonville?"

I laughed. "Quite a lot of excitement, apparently, and my house was sort of implicated, or at least in the mix."

"What happened?"

I told her what I knew of the robbery, and how the thief had run across the cornfield, and how he couldn't be found for several hours.

"Couldn't be found? In Burtonville? Running around carrying paintings? That doesn't make a lot of sense," Natalie suggested.

"I agree. And Ashley thought he might have hidden in my basement. You know there's an access door outside in the yard."

"Hid in your basement? What? When was this?"

"Oh …" I tried to remember what Ashley had said. Had she mentioned when it all happened? "Um," I finished lamely.

"I'm Googling!" Natalie chirped, and I could hear her fingers tapping away on her computer keyboard. "Theft, Burtonville, Paintings …" There was a pause and more tapping. "The guy was killed? Whoa!"

"Yes, apparently, he got hit by a car." I avoided saying or even thinking the word squashed.

"Wait. This happened about ten days ago," Natalie said. "How did you not know?"

"Good question," I answered. "Are you sure? Ten days?"

"That's what this article says. 'Art Theft In Burtonville Stuns Residents.' This has gotta be it."

"But ..." I started, and then paused.

"This is crazy!" I could tell Natalie had found another online article. "The officer chased him, but he was missing for like four hours. Where could he have been hiding?"

"I'm guessing in the cornfield. The stalks are pretty tall."

"But with paintings? In a cornfield?"

"I think it's even crazier I didn't read or hear about it. But I was packing and dealing with the realtor in Peoria and then Duffy—" I broke off.

"I think the basement's more likely," Natalie commented.

"But it was supposed to be locked. The realtor said she would put a lock on it, although there isn't one there now."

"Maybe she didn't do it."

"Oh, she definitely did, but truthfully, I hadn't been 'round to look since we closed on the house," I confessed. "I just came and dropped stuff off."

And Duffy planted chrysanthemums. Suddenly I felt rather depressed.

"Well, it's over anyway," Natalie said.

"Yeah." I sat down with a thump in a kitchen chair. All at once, the mess in the living room seemed less like a project and more like exactly what it was—a mess. And I had stuff in storage, and furniture to be delivered, and the second bedroom still needed a onceover. The paint was badly chipped on some of the walls.

As always, Natalie was tuned in to my moods. "Hey! I've got exams next week, but how 'bout I come to visit the week after? It would be only for the weekend, and only if you promise not to go nuts trying to get the house ready before I get there. I saw it before you moved in, remember? Nothing's going to surprise me."

"I'd love to have you, my dear. Can I go a little nuts?"

"No nuts," said Natalie firmly, and laughed.

"Okay, no nuts," I answered, crossing my fingers.

"Uncross your fingers."

"Natalie, you're impossible!"

"Ooh, I hope so." My stepdaughter giggled and clicked off.

Shaking my head, I stuffed my cell phone in my pocket, fed the last piece of pizza to Rowdy and dropped the box in the recycling bin.

"C'mon, my man. Time for a walk. I know we already had one, but this will be good for you."

Rowdy opened one eye and then closed it again.

"Rowdy! Come *on*! Think of all the food we ate!" I reached down and grabbed his collar, giving it a tug for good measure. Honestly, we were together on a beautiful night and all he wanted to do was sleep?

Rowdy heaved himself to his feet, yawned and shook, and then followed me to the door, where I snagged his leash and snapped it on his collar. We walked outside into the warm gloaming and I took a deep breath, feeling a measure of my uneasiness wash away. A stupid fight with my not-boyfriend, an art theft that really wasn't relevant to anything, and a big house project? What big house project? It was just a series of small projects. The sort I'd done many times before. All doable; all fine.

I stretched my shoulders and began to stroll east, away from the dog-hating Paulsens. Across the street, an older gray sedan was parked under a maple tree. The windows were cracked open and I could see a man behind the wheel. I raised my hand in greeting—small town friendliness. In response, he slumped down in his seat and turned his face away.

So much for small town friendliness. I finished the rest of my walk feeling sullen and irritated, and my peace vanished.

Chapter Four

Despite my gloomy mood the evening before, I awakened the next day with a new surge of energy, and I had two walls in the living room sanded before I even sat down to breakfast. Natalie called to tell me she might be able to come for her visit earlier than planned, the furniture store called to set up a date to deliver my new couch and chairs and I got a brainstorm about putting up a martin house in the section of the yard where Duffy's chrysanthemums were planted. In fact, why not make a little secret garden? That idea led to a foray into fencing options, but soon I was back at the drywall, which was turning out very well—almost professional looking. All in all, a satisfactory start to the morning.

At 11AM, I took a break, fetched a cup of coffee from the coffeemaker—finding it was another of the morning's accomplishments—and telephoned my realtor.

"Hey!" Loretta greeted me. "You're not sick of your house already, are you?"

"Not at all. In fact, I've got so many projects lined up that I'll have to stay here another hundred years to get them all done."

"Well, that's good," said Loretta. "All fun projects, I hope?"

"Always," I answered. "But I called for a different reason. You know the outside door that leads to the basement?"

"Of course."

"I wondered about the lock. Remember we—"

"Oh, yes," Loretta said instantly. "We put a lock on for a little extra security. Is everything okay?"

"I think so. I just wanted to ask where the lock went?"

"Where it went? It's not there?"

I frowned. "No, it's not. I can get another one, but I wondered if you took the one that we bought. The key's still in my kitchen, hanging on the nail where we left it."

"That's odd. Hang on a second." Canned music started up, and while I waited I gazed out the window at what would someday be my secret garden. A bench and a willow privacy fence perhaps. Some sort of umbrella for shade? The weather was staying warm for autumn, but I knew it was a matter of time before the temps began to fall. The secret garden would be a great spring project.

"Marianne?" Loretta was back on the line. "Sorry for the wait. I asked Jason, and it turns out we have the lock here. When he went to take down the key box after you bought the house, apparently he thought the basement padlock was one of ours and he brought it back, too. Who knows why? The kid is giving me high blood pressure. Yesterday he put a For Sale sign in front of the wrong house. It was an interesting phone conversation when the owners called."

I laughed. "I can imagine."

"I'll get the lock out to you. I apologize. We have the other key here, too."

"No need to bring the lock back. I'll mail you my key and then maybe you can use the lock for something else. I'll buy a new one." I really wanted to start all over. New lock; new keys; everything mine.

"You sure?" asked Loretta. "We don't use that kind of lock for anything, but maybe it'd come in handy someday. Really, I don't know what Jason was thinking. He's the perfect example of why you shouldn't hire your nephew."

I laughed again. "Honestly, it's no problem. I'm going to one of those big box stores for supplies, anyhow. I'll buy another." I hesitated. "Did you hear about the robbery here?"

"Oh, good God," Loretta exclaimed. "Did you have a break-in? Honestly, if Jason had anything to do with that, he's sacked."

"No," I hurried to answer. "It was at a different house. Some paintings were stolen."

"Oh, that. Yes, I knew about it. So strange. There was an officer from the sheriff's department right in the home doing some shopping. Weird coincidence. And then the thief got killed."

I swallowed. "A neighbor told me. I hadn't heard. Too busy packing up to move, I guess. The guy was on his cell phone and ran out into the road."

"Yes," answered Loretta. "And I think it wasn't just paintings that were taken. The woman having the sale was quite elderly and didn't have a good inventory. I bet her insurance company is having fits." Then, "Hang on, Marianne," Loretta said, and again I was on hold. Soon, she was back. "I've got another call I better take. Anything else I can do for you today?"

"Nope, don't think so." I hung up feeling much better about several things, and added padlock on the shopping list.

I walked out and took a turn around the yard, scoping out the area for my martin house and private garden, then I went back inside and called my friend, Louise, in Peoria.

"Hi, stranger!" she said. "Good to hear your voice."

31

I frowned. Had I been so out of touch that my best friend was now greeting me as 'stranger?' "Hi, Louise," I answered. "Wondered if you're free for early dinner? I'm going to make a trip your way for a bunch of supplies."

"Sure!" answered Louise. "How's the house coming?"

"Coming," I said shortly. "As soon as the living room's done, I'll have you out and maybe we can do a cookout. Right now, things are in too much of a mess. I haven't unpacked too well, and I've got no furniture except what's in my kitchen."

"I feel a poem coming on," said Louise.

"Stop it. There's no tragedy to be had here. Honestly. Do you want to have dinner?"

"Of course!" she answered. "I've got a class until 3:00. Sometime after that?"

I glanced at the clock. Maybe I *was* too holed up here in Burtonville. I'd forgotten what day it was. Of course, Louise taught on Tuesdays and Thursdays.

"4:30?" I answered. "That'll give me time to make a couple of calls, get cleaned up and drive in to do my shopping. I'm not sure what's become of the cable company, and I have no Internet. I've got to call and rattle their cage."

"No Internet?" Louise sounded shocked. "You better get that call made, girl!"

I laughed. "On it. See you at 4:30."

I grabbed a quick lunch, called the cable company and made suitably urgent noises, then took a shower, gave Rowdy a quick pat and hit the road. At the home store, I bought paint and some new paint brushes; took a look at options for outdoor benches and fencing; checked out the wallpaper designs. No knights available. I'd have to go online to search if the cable company ever showed up. I also found a heavy duty padlock for my basement door. I contemplated simply replacing the knob, but it was an unusual design that looked antique and I wanted to see about having a new key made instead. Time for that after other projects were done. In the meantime, the padlock would do the job.

I checked out, and as I loaded my purchases into the Prius I thought of Duffy and debated phoning him to see if he would like to join Louise and me. I decided against it. It was 4:00, so any invitation would seem like an afterthought, and he was probably at work, anyway. Besides, I was still smarting from the long silence, and I didn't feel like starting the conversation with an apology—which I knew I would be tempted to do, even if there was nothing to apologize for.

Grumpily, I climbed in the car and drove to *Fibber McGee's*, Louise's and my favorite seafood restaurant. Soon we were sipping Margaritas and nibbling on shrimp cocktail and exchanging news and gossip.

"I thought Duffy might be with you," Louise commented, and when I frowned, she added, "Uh oh. What's going on?"

"To tell you the truth, I don't really know. He's gone completely silent—doesn't call, nothing."

"Why don't you call him?"

"I don't want to," I said stubbornly, but felt a twinge of guilt. "I have the feeling he's mad about something and I'll just end up apologizing, and I'm not sorry. At least, I can't think of anything to be sorry for."

"Well, you did break his heart," Louise commented mildly.

I slapped my hand down on the table harder than I meant to, bouncing the silverware and making the couple at the next table glance over at us. I straightened my fork, feeling my face flushing. Louise grinned.

I grimaced. "Sorry. But, Louise, I did *not* break his heart. Duffy and I are *friends*, nothing more … or we were, anyway. I never led him to believe anything else. He knew I was moving, he came to see the house and didn't like it—fine; it's a mess and I agree with that—but then one day, before I moved in, he and I were there and he was helping me and he planted these beautiful yellow mums, which he knows I love …" To my horror, I suddenly felt as if I might be getting tears in my eyes.

Louise was staring out the window, so I took a quick swipe at my face with my napkin to remove any offending liquid.

"He knows I love yellow chrysanthemums," I continued, "and we were having what I thought was a pretty good day, and then something happened—I have no idea what—and he went storming off. Not a word from him since then."

"He didn't even say goodbye?"

"Well, yes, he did say goodbye, but it was kind of stiff and angry-sounding."

"That's rather rude. And not really like Duffy." Louise took a swallow of her Margarita.

"I know," I said. "He was unhappy I decided to leave Peoria, but I never thought we wouldn't stay friends or anything. I thought we could be like we were before, except I would be in a different house. I dunno. Men are complicated."

"Yes, they surely are." Louise smiled, but then she leaned across the table and touched the back of my hand. "Are you ever going to consider remarrying? Or even having another romantic relationship?"

"Are *you*?" I shot back, but Louise, who knew where this was heading—in fact, we'd had that same conversation a dozen times—didn't take the bait.

"I'm at least considering it," she answered lightly. "Looking around. But Brian left just a couple

35

of years ago, and you've been a widow for nearly a decade."

I sat back in my chair and sighed. "Let's drop it. Maybe I'll end up calling Duffy, or maybe he'll end up calling me. Or maybe I'll never hear from him again and it'll all be a big fat mystery. In the meantime, we've got shrimp cocktail to eat and fish tacos on the way. Let's not waste our evening talking about our love lives, or our no-love lives. Or whatever it is we're talking about."

Louise smiled. "Oui, Madame!" She raised her glass. "To the House on Beale Street."

"À la maison!" I replied.

Two hours later, Louise had expressed proper surprise and curiosity about the robbery and my basement, we had devoured everything on our plates and even split a caramel crunch ice cream pie, and we finally bid each other farewell, promising to meet again for the *Fibber*'s all-you-can-eat crab buffet. I took a cup of decaf to go and sipped it as I drove along the road for Burtonville, humming along with Oldies on the radio and thinking of wallpaper and chrysanthemums.

Finally, I picked up my cell phone—I knew I was eventually going to do it—and dialed Duffy's number. I got his voicemail, and I hesitated for a moment, wondering what message to leave.

"Hey, it's me," I finally said, as I turned on to Beale Street and started down the road toward my house. "Thought I'd call and check in. Hope everything's good—" I stopped abruptly.

Someone was in my yard. Not only in my yard, but standing at my basement door, and he appeared to be reaching for the door handle. I threw my phone in the passenger seat, slammed on my brakes and stopped in front of the house, not even bothering to turn into the driveway. I climbed out, sprinted around my car and across the yard.

The man looked up, saw me charging toward him and stepped backward, looking alarmed. I saw he held a flat package or envelope under his arm.

"Can I help you with something?" I shouted as I neared him, anger making my voice shake. *I leave for an afternoon and what happens?* "What do you want?"

Chapter Five

"Um, sorry ma'am. I'm Kevin Flynn from Central and Mid-State Cable. I'm here to hook up your service."

"In the basement?" I was still shouting, but I couldn't help it.

"No one answered the door ..."

"I wasn't *home*." I went from shouting to gritting my teeth. Duane used to say it was a good time to pull out the white flag when I began gritting my teeth.

"Right." And perhaps Kevin Flynn was getting the picture after all, because he took two careful steps away from me.

"Wait right there!" I headed toward my car, then turned around when I was halfway across the lawn. "Do *not* leave."

"No, ma'am," he said, clutching his envelope.

I pulled the Prius into the garage, retrieved my purse and keys, and went back to the serviceman, who was still standing in my yard, looking a bit shell-shocked. I was slightly mollified by the sight of the van parked along the road. It had a bright red **C & M-S Cable** logo painted on the side. I kind of wished I'd spotted that before I started yelling, but what was he doing trying to get in the basement, anyway?

Half an hour later, I was the rest of the way mollified. He gave me a sheaf of papers to read, checked my cable hook-up, and promised to have it up and running by the next morning. "You called and said it was urgent," he commented, a bit defensively, I thought.

"I was promised two-day turnaround for my hook-up, and it's been longer than two days," I shot back, and he winced.

"I'm very sorry for the confusion, ma'am. I was looking for a doorbell. I thought I was at the back door. I was … well, you said it was urgent."

That was reasonable, and actually believable. I decided to give him a break. "And I'm sorry I was alarmed."

"Just sign here, ma'am." He handed me a pen. "I believe our representative explained you might have an evening visit."

"Yes, you're right." He wasn't going to let me off the hook, apparently. I signed, signed again, handed him his papers and a check. "Thank you for making a special trip out. I appreciate it."

He gave me a look, polite but not quite friendly. "Tomorrow morning. Cable up and running," he repeated.

"Thanks," I said again, and he made his exit.

I watched him walk out to the van and climb in, then I went to the garage to fetch my shopping bags. I rummaged through my purchases until I found the padlock and marched around to the back door.

Moments later, the lock was snapped in place. With a sigh of satisfaction, I took the keys and packing materials inside and tossed them on the kitchen table, then unloaded the rest of my items from the car, piling the paint in the living room. First thing the next morning, I would put on the base coat, then my lavender wallpaper could go up. I gave myself a pleased little shake, feeling happy and fulfilled. Lock back on the basement, living room coming around, and Internet soon to be available. What else could a girl want?

It was at that moment that I remembered Duffy and my heart dropped down to the tip of my toes. I was leaving a voicemail when I drove up the road, but what happened when I saw the cable company at the basement door? Had I signed off, or was I in mid-message? I looked for my cell phone in my purse, in the back pocket of my jeans, and under the table, then remembered tossing it on the car seat. I ran back out to the garage to retrieve it, vaulting over Rowdy, who was lying by the door looking confused, trying to figure out whether I was coming home or going back out again.

Holding my breath, I checked the display. There were three missed calls and two voicemails, all from Duffy.

I carried the phone back in the house and stared at it for a moment. So much for the friendly, "Hi," and, "Long time no talk." This was not going to be fun. But I owed him a call back, for several reasons, and it was no time to be a coward. Hadn't I taken on the cable guy? If I could do that, I could handle Duffy.

Even so, I sighed. Did I want things to be back the way they were, when I was in Peoria; plain and untroubled? No, I answered myself firmly. I wanted to be in my new place with my new things and new things to do, but I wanted all the see-sawing back and forth to stop. Happy one minute; unhappy the next. It was unsettling, and not like me.

I gripped the phone and dialed Duffy's number. He answered on the first ring, without a hello. "Are you all right?"

I smiled. As irritating as he could be sometimes, it was good to hear his voice. "Yes, I'm completely fine. I'm sorry about cutting off my message. I thought … I wasn't expecting the cable guy to show up. I was just getting home from shopping and there he was."

"Cutting me off? Actually, you left a three minute voicemail, and there was a good deal of commotion in the background. Yelling, more like."

"I'm sorry." I rolled my eyes and looked at the ceiling. *Could things get any worse?* "I guess the call didn't disconnect. A mix-up, is all. How are you?"

"I'm fine," he answered, and it was that comment that made me realize how really upset he was. Duffy's definition of the fastest way to quash a conversation was that answer. "Fine."

Uncertain how to respond, or really what to say next—a first for Duffy and me—I said, "Good!" and then there was a long silence.

When Duffy said, "Well," the precursor for signing off, I blurted out, "Duffy, what's wrong? I don't understand what's happened. Did I do something? If so, I don't know what it is."

I imagined him on the other end of the line, his tall, loose frame and his probably-slightly-rumpled jacket. If I knew him as once I thought I did, he was pacing back and forth in his study, looking out the window and running his hands over his books. He could never stand still when he talked on his phone.

He cleared his throat and I waited. "I'm doing some thinking, is all. Just need to get through it."

"About me?" I asked hesitantly.

"Well, more about me, really."

"Did something happen?" I asked again, but he didn't answer.

"How's the house coming?" he said instead.

"Fine." I winced. This was awful. "That is, slowly, but it's coming. I'll be hanging wallpaper day after tomorrow. And then the living room furniture comes. I should have my Internet up in the morning."

"Good. 'Progress lies not in enhancing what is, but in advancing toward what will be,'" he quoted.

I laughed. Duffy wasn't a big fan of Kahlil Gibran, but Gibran always seemed to have a passage that fit the occasion, and Duffy was an avid lover of the 1960s counterculture. He had shelves of books about artists and 1960s lore. "That does it," I announced. "I'm getting you that CD of Gibran readings after all."

"No! Don't!" he exclaimed, and I laughed again.

Better. It was getting a bit better. "I met my neighbor, and found a good pizza place," I offered.

"Good," he said. "But, Marianne, I'm going to sign off. I've had a tough day, and am likely to have another tomorrow. I want to kick back for a bit."

"What—?" I began, but he broke in.

"Just take my word for it. Have a good night, then, okay?"

"Okay," I answered, and heard his quick, "So long."

I sat down at the kitchen table and set my phone down in front of me. Why did, and how did, things get so thorny? I sighed, then looked up when Rowdy wandered by and stared at the door next to my bedroom. The inside door to the basement.

"What's up, my man?" I asked.

My dog turned his mournful face to mine, and then went back to his staring. I frowned.

"What's up?" I repeated.

Rowdy didn't answer, of course, but after a moment he turned around once and, with a groan, lay down with his back against the door. I looked at him closely, then shook my head. For a moment, it had almost seemed—almost—as if he were guarding the entrance. But against what? The mice that were no doubt camped down there amidst all the flotsam and jetsam that needed to be shoveled out?

I sighed again and got up from the table. It was early, but my body and my brain were telling me it was time to give up for the day. I liked to read in bed until I drifted off to sleep, and tonight was a good night for it. I walked past Rowdy and gave him a pat, and for good measure, I reached out and turned the basement doorknob. Tightly locked. Shrugging, I went on to the bedroom, climbed over the tumbled boxes stacked near the closet—my discard pile— and began changing for bed. I gave the boxes a sullen glance. The stack was getting huge, and I thought I had done a reasonable job of cleaning out before I left Peoria. Apparently not. I needed to get a dumpster and a larger recycling bin. Something else for the To Do list.

After a few minutes, Rowdy sauntered in. "Ready to turn in for the night, Mr. Bear?" I asked him.

Rowdy shook and flopped down next to the bed. I snagged my paperback off the bedside stand, put on my reading glasses, and lost myself in the fun of a really good mystery story, replete with a brave heroine, a handsome but inaccessible lover, and a faux Stradivarius. Almost without realizing it, I began drifting off to sleep, so I set the book and my glasses on the bedside table and closed my eyes.

I was awakened by what sounded like something falling.

For a moment, I lay staring into the dark trying to figure out what I'd heard. Then I wondered where Rowdy had gone. I couldn't hear his rumbling snores or feel his presence in the room. I turned on the lamp and when I didn't see him, went out to the hallway. There he was, just as before, lying with his back against the basement door. He didn't appear much alarmed—in fact, his eyes were half-closed— but I felt a small frisson of alarm nonetheless. Reaching, I tried the door knob again. Locked. What had made that sound? It seemed as if it might have been a can tipping off a shelf and then rolling, and it also seemed to have come from the basement. A mouse wouldn't do such a thing, I was quite certain, unless it was the size of a Beagle. I hoped I didn't have a raccoon or a squirrel or something. But how would it have gotten in?

I stood for several minutes, straining my ears for any further noises, but all remained quiet. Soon Rowdy began to snore gently, so I went back in the bedroom, telling myself at least a dozen times that either I'd imagined the noise, or else I hadn't imagined it, but it was something innocuous. Besides, anything bumping around in the basement would have Rowdy to deal with if it tried to come upstairs, and that would involve pushing him out of the way to get the door open. No raccoon or squirrel would be able to manage that. Finally, feeling vaguely comforted, I went back to sleep.

However, I did not feel comforted the following morning when I took Rowdy out for his visit to the yard. As I walked past the outside door to the basement, I saw that the padlock was gone.

Chapter Six

Although I knew whatever had transpired in my basement the night before was probably long past, and whatever or whoever had perpetrated it was probably long gone, I ran inside and phoned 9-1-1. I assured the dispatcher that I had not gone down to the basement to check, but that all seemed quiet and there was no sign of an intruder. Then, while I waited for the sheriff's department to arrive, I fed Rowdy and changed out of my painting clothes into something more presentable. To boost my spirits, I poured a cup of coffee and added a generous scoop of raw sugar. The day was not starting off well, and I felt alternately furious and uneasy.

For the noise, there might have been an explanation—a mouse or a rat even—but the missing padlock was seriously upsetting. Unless said mouse or rat had suddenly grown super-rodent teeth, it was a human that had removed the lock from my door; probably with a pair of bolt cutters. I took my cup of coffee and went back outside, surveying the door from a distance. It seemed as if the grass at the basement threshold had been packed down or trampled, but who knew? There had certainly been plenty of people in the yard—including myself and Duffy.

A sheriff's car drew up on the street, and I hurried inside to usher two uniformed officers through my front door.

"Marianne Reed?"

"Yes, that's me."

"I'm Officer Stanton from the sheriff's department, and this is Officer Willet. You had a break-in?"

"I think so."

I led them back outside to the basement door and explained what had happened while Officer Stanton jotted notes down on a small tablet and Officer Willet walked the perimeter of my garage.

"When did you put the padlock on?"

"Yesterday evening around 8PM. I bought it because I thought the door needed one and the realtor mistakenly removed the one that had been on the door before."

"You just moved here?" He glanced around the yard and spied Rowdy, looking for all the world like a large hairy lump snoring away under his tree.

"Yes. I'm still getting settled."

"Mind if we look around inside the basement?"

"Not at all."

Officer Stanton turned the door knob and the two men started downstairs. I stood at the head of the stairs and watched them peruse the cluttered space. Officer Willet glanced up at me. "Is anything missing?"

"I have absolutely no idea," I responded. "It's a mess down there, and I've been concentrating on renovating other parts of the house. I figured I would tackle this last."

"Lots of storage," he commented. "Nice and dry."

"I figured I'd put those shelves to good use, but first I've got to sort everything the previous owners left behind."

"None of these things are yours?"

"None of them. It was all there when I came."

"Any idea if there's something valuable down here?"

"I doubt it. I can't think what it would be."

"Come on down," said Officer Willet, and I joined the officers in the basement.

"I can't see any signs of vandalism, can you?" Officer Stanton asked. "And you said you can't tell what, if anything, might be missing?"

"No, I can't see that anything is damaged, and I'm afraid I couldn't say if anything was stolen. I don't know what's down here."

The officers looked around a few more minutes, gazing into corners and eyeing the shelves. "Okay," Officer Stanton said and led the way back outside. I shut off the light and closed the door while he made a few more notes.

"Did your dog bark?"

"Last night? Bark?" I turned and looked at Rowdy. "That dog? I'm not sure he knows how."

Officer Stanton laughed, showing even, white teeth. He was a good looking man, with dark, curly hair and chocolate brown eyes. He pointed at Rowdy. "Is he friendly?"

"Sure," I said, and he walked over to kneel next to my somnolent canine companion.

"Hey, fellow." He scratched Rowdy behind the right ear, and Rowdy lifted his head, half opened one eye, yawned, and went back to sleep. The officer laughed again. "Great guy."

"Thanks!" I had liked Officer Stanton on the spot, and I liked him even more now.

He stood up. "Sorry for the trouble here. I'll put together a report, and we'll spread the word around. There was a theft in the area not too long ago. I don't see how this is related, but it's worth keeping in mind. If you notice anything unusual, call the station."

"I'll do that," I said. "Thanks for coming over."

"You're very welcome."

The officers went out to their car and drove away, and I returned to the kitchen. What was left of my cup of coffee had gotten cold, so I poured another cup and sat down at the table.

I debated what to do about getting another lock. There was a hardware store in town, but I wasn't sure what selection of padlocks they might have and I wanted to get one with a hidden shackle this time. I scolded myself for not buying a better lock to begin with. But how could I have known someone would want to get in so badly that they'd cut it off? And what in the world were they after? The basement appeared to be full of nothing but junk. Nonetheless, I didn't like the idea of people going willy-nilly in and out of my house. It was a decidedly creepy feeling. Another trip to Peoria was in order, but I changed back into my work clothes and painted the basecoat on my new drywall first. It could be curing while I ran my errands.

After I finished painting, I puttered around the kitchen for a while, got another cup of coffee, put together some minestrone in my slow cooker and refilled Rowdy's water bowl. I was going to get my purse and head out to the garage when there was a knock on front door. It was Ashley Midden.

"Hi!" she said, smiling. "Saw you had the sheriff here earlier. Is everything okay?"

"Oh, yes," I answered. "I had a little trouble, but it's all right. No big deal."

"Really?" She waited, looking worried, and I finally stood back and invited her in.

"Don't touch the walls. It's wet paint."

"Okay," she said. "Things are coming right along. Wallpaper next?"

"Wallpaper next," I agreed, watching her perch on her sawhorse seat. "Coffee?" I asked.

Ashley shook her head. "Not today. I can't stay too long. Just thought I'd make sure you were okay."

"Yup. All okay," I repeated. I knew Ashley was hoping for details, and I finally relented. "Someone broke in to my basement, but nothing's stolen that I know of, and nothing damaged."

"Wow!" she exclaimed. "I hope that man …"

"What man?" I asked sharply.

"The one that was here earlier," said Ashley.

"Earlier?" I asked. "Yesterday?"

"No, he was here a few days before you arrived. I saw him when I was walking over to introduce myself, but then I thought you had company so I didn't stop by. I didn't realize you hadn't moved in yet. I don't know who it was. He was out in your yard."

"Probably the realtor's nephew," I commented. "He was here taking down the For Sale sign and so on."

"You mean Jason?" asked Ashley, and I looked at her in surprise. "You used Loretta Jackson, right? Yeah, her nephew's Jason. He works for her."

I wondered if there was anyone Ashley didn't know, and said as much. She laughed. "Loretta does a lot of the realty work around here. Most people know her. She's good folks, but her nephew's a bit of a loose cannon. He went to school in Prairie City, but dropped out before he graduated high school. But it wasn't Jason I saw that day. It was someone else. Kind of an older man—heavy set, balding. A stranger. I saw him try your basement door, but it was locked. I was walking up the drive with cookies, you know, and he seemed kind of startled to see me. He went round the other side of the garage and drove away, and I went home. I thought it was kind of strange."

"Hmm." I was puzzled. "What kind of a car did he have?" *That basement. The whole world seems to want to get down there*, I thought.

Ashley shrugged. "I didn't notice his car. Do you know him?"

"I don't think so," I answered. "I know people who look sort of like that, I guess. But I can't think what they'd be doing here."

"Maybe you should tell the sheriff."

I hesitated. "Oh, no, I don't think so. It's all sort of a vague coincidence, and I don't want to get everyone all stirred up. There isn't enough information to actually report anything. Besides, for some reason, I think last night's disturbance was kids or something."

"Kids?" Ashley looked startled and gave me a wary glance. "Why do you think that?"

"I don't know. Just a thought."

"The kids around here are pretty good." Ashley stood up. "It was probably that man. I better go," she said abruptly.

I was so taken aback that I was motionless for a moment. Then, "Of course," I said, and walked with her to the door. Instead of lingering in the driveway as she had last time, she seemed in a hurry to leave, and I wondered if I had offended her somehow.

"I was going to make a run to the craft store later this week. Would you like to go along with me?" I offered.

Ashley was already hustling away, but she stopped and looked over her shoulder. "That would be fun. Let me know when."

"I don't have your phone number, I don't think," I called, but she was already out of earshot.

I shrugged, wondering what was going on. 'Perplexity is the beginning of knowledge,' I unconsciously quoted Gibran, and then thought of Duffy. I wondered what Duffy would make of the day's happenings, and decided not to tell him. If I talked to him again. *When* I talked to him again. Honestly, things were getting more complicated rather than less.

I checked to make sure my Internet connection worked. It did—no need to have the cable company back. Then I called Louise, but got her voicemail. So I made the trip to Peoria without any plans for a dinner date, and I bought the best lock I could find, a high-security stainless steel one with a hidden shackle. It felt heavy and solid in my hand. No standard bolt cutter was going to harm this baby. Humming to myself and feeling quite satisfied, I drove home and took my lock around to the back yard.

"Try and get that off, whoever you are," I grumbled as I put the lock on the hasp and stood back to survey my work.

I took the new set of keys in the house and hung them on the nail, threw the old key on the table to send to Loretta, and set the table for an early supper, putting out a bowl for my minestrone, some brown bread, and a chocolate cupcake I picked up in Peoria. Just as I was sitting down at the table, my cell phone rang—Louise calling me back.

"Darn it! I missed you!" she said, when I told her about my second trip to Peoria, and why.

"Don't worry. At the rate things are going, I'll be visiting the home improvement store a lot. We'll meet up next time."

"What's the deal with that basement of yours?" my friend asked, and I shook my head.

"Beats me," I answered, wandering to the living room with the phone under my ear. "I wouldn't want to be down there with all that junk." I touched the new paint. Dry and good to go. Tomorrow, wallpaper; those pretty lavender rolls that I'd been saving. Suddenly, my basement problems seemed not all that important. "It all feels like a string of coincidences to me. I'm sure this is the end of it."

I looked out the picture window at Beale Street and saw a gray sedan creeping by. Speaking of coincidences. Frowning, I went to the other window and watched until the vehicle was out of sight. Was it the same one I saw parked before? I tried to remember what make the car was, but to my annoyance, I drew a blank.

"Marianne?" Louise asked loudly.

"Sorry. I got distracted for a minute. What did you say?"

"I asked if you'd heard from Duffy."

"Well, I got him on the phone. He's still acting strange, but we did manage to talk a little bit. It was nice." My cell phone vibrated, and I held it away from my ear to look at the display. A text message from Natalie read, **Get ready! I'm coming to visit on Friday!** "And speaking of nice," I went on, "Natalie's coming this weekend. So I better get booking tomorrow and get her room fixed up."

"Great! And I don't care if your place is still a mess. I'm coming for dinner. I can't miss seeing Natalie."

"Okay," I answered. "Hopefully, I'll have furniture!"

"Well, while you're booking to get Natalie's room done, tell the furniture store to book it and bring your living room stuff."

"On it," I said. "I'm excited! My first house party."

"Look out, Burtonville!" laughed Louise.

Chapter Seven

I climbed out of bed early the next day, and after checking my outside basement door to make sure the padlock was still there (it was), and tending to Rowdy, I took my breakfast coffee to the living room, dragged out my wallpapering paraphernalia, and began putting up the lavender paper.

Soon three of the walls were covered with the beautiful wallcovering I'd picked out especially for the room, and I knew I'd chosen exactly the right thing. The living room looked as if it had been lit with dawn, and the subtle pattern in the paper reminded me of clouds. I loved it. It was tempting to drag one of my kitchen chairs out to the living room to sit and admire what I'd done, but I had other things to take care of. I wanted to look at benches and fencing for my secret garden, but first I needed to get Natalie's room squared away. Later on, I would paint the accent wall in the living room. I'd chosen an ice blue, and I couldn't wait to see how it turned out.

I tackled Natalie's room first. The bed was already set up, so I pushed it into the corner and carried boxes to my bedroom to get them out of the way. Then I unpacked and hung curtains, stowed extra sheets and blankets in the corner of the closet, and began unloading office items to arrange my desk. The tall floor lamp was in the living room, so I brought that and my laptop computer in. Next was to hang Natalie's pictures. The knights-on-horseback border would have to wait. After her visit, I'd move everything out away from the walls and paint. Maybe while I was searching for benches, I'd do some digging for wallpaper borders, too.

I stacked Natalie's collection of beloved photos—cats in various poses of play and sleep—on the bed, then hung them one by one neatly on the walls using tiny nails. I unwrapped the picture of her mother, Iris, that she had on her bedside stand back home in Peoria, set it next to the lamp, and stood back to admire my handiwork. My desk was next. Going back to the boxes, I took out a pencil cup Natalie made when she was in middle school and put that out, along with my stapler and a tape dispenser. Then I stood up and frowned. I was missing a box—one where I had packed a picture of Duane and me in San Diego, both of us grinning; Duane with his lips pressed to my hair. We'd asked a young man to take a picture of us in front of the pool at Balboa Park, and he'd snapped a candid shot that became one of my favorites. It always sat on my desk next to my computer at the old house.

I went out to the living room and looked around, but I'd distributed to other rooms in the house all the boxes that were left there by the movers. Then I went in the bedroom and looked through all the unpacked cartons—even the ones I knew held Christmas ornaments, wreaths and a string of solar lights.

After that, I sorted through all the cartons, packing paper and rubble piled in my bedroom for the dumpster and recycling. Then I went out to the garage and dragged out the few boxes of tools I'd left on the workbench, just in case. Nothing. I was sure I recalled what the box looked like. It was flat and rectangular, and the photograph was the only thing in it, except for a piece of old quilting that I set my laptop computer on to keep it from sliding around. The quilting was nothing important; in fact, I intended to pitch it when the moving was done, but I used it to pad the picture to keep it from getting damaged. What I didn't remember was unloading the box from my car, or seeing it anywhere after the moving van left.

I went back in the house and thumped down at the kitchen table, my joy in my pretty lavender living room dampened. I really wanted that photo. Was there any chance of finding the digital copy and making a duplicate? I had no idea where it might be. I felt tears begin to slide down my face. I wiped them away. Wiped them away again. Blew my nose. Grabbed the tissue box and set it near me.

Then I had a really good cry. I cried until my throat hurt and my nose was plugged. I cried until my head ached. I wanted Duane with his kiss on my hair, and if I couldn't have him, I wanted that photo that gave me such joy. I cried about everything until I was sick of crying, and finally I managed to stop. Then, blowing my nose and mopping my face, I fetched a cup of sweet tea and called Natalie.

"Mummy!"

"Hello, sweetie. Are you busy?"

"You've been crying. What's wrong?"

I smiled. Trust Natalie to instantly pick up on my mood. "Oh …" What *was* really wrong? I wanted my photo back, and I wanted things to settle and be regular and sort of normal. Not completely normal—never that—but less weird and hard to figure out. "I can't find something," I admitted. "It's upsetting me."

"What?"

"That photo of me and your dad. The one we took in San Diego …"

"I remember. The one you had on your desk. It's lost?"

"Yes, I think so," I felt my voice start to quaver and actually pinched my arm to make myself stop.

For Heaven's sake, how could there be any moisture left anywhere in my body?

"That's terrible!" Natalie exclaimed. "No wonder you're sad. But you know, it probably isn't really lost. It's just misplaced. When I come, we'll look for it and we'll find it."

"You think? I'm worried it maybe got thrown away. I've tossed scads of stuff."

"It didn't get tossed. I know we'll find it," she answered firmly. "Besides, I'm positive I've got it on my old external hard drive. If it doesn't show up, I'll dig it out and make you another copy. No worries."

"That's very sweet," I said. "I feel better."

"You sure that's all that's wrong?"

"That's mostly it. I'm a little melancholy today for some reason."

"When I come we'll have ice cream every night," answered my intrepid stepdaughter, and that made me start to laugh.

"Deal," I said, and we signed off.

Feeling substantially better, I finished my tea and made another foray to the garage on the off chance I'd perhaps overlooked a box or two, but the missing photograph did not make an appearance. Frowning, I went back in the house, pulled out the can of ice blue paint and my roller, and smoothed paint over the accent wall in the living room. Then I put up a barricade so Rowdy wouldn't rub against the wall and turn himself into a giant light blue Smurf, and I went to the bedroom to change. It wasn't too late in the day. I decided what might cheer me up would be to make that trip to Peoria to the craft store. I would ask Ashley to come along.

Soon I was walking along the street toward her house, recalling her odd behavior when she visited the day before and hoping my showing up on her doorstep wasn't going to be an uncomfortable encounter. Ashley's house was pretty and compact, painted a sunshine yellow with window boxes stuffed full of brightly colored annuals—geraniums and marigolds and brilliant blue forget-me-nots. I resolved to get some gardening advice from her. Despite my love of chrysanthemums, I never had a lot of luck with them. They usually only ended up lasting one season.

I lifted my hand to knock, but before I could do so, the door opened and I was greeted by a tall, gangly boy with a shock of dark hair, cut long and curling wildly around his face.

"Oh!" He looked at me in surprise.

"I'm sorry. I was just about to knock," I said. "Are you Joe?"

Before he could answer, I heard Ashley say, "Who's that, Cole?" and she walked around the corner, wiping her hands on a towel. "Marianne!" she exclaimed. She shot a look at Cole. "What a surprise to see you here. She's our neighbor, Cole.

The one who lives in front of the cornfield. Marianne, this is Cole, Joe's friend."

I smiled, but Cole didn't acknowledge the introduction. Instead, he looked away and backed into the house. Ashley gestured for me to come in.

"How's your day been?" Ashley asked, and I saw Cole edge out of sight. For a moment, I thought he looked furtive, but I couldn't imagine why.

"Going pretty good," I answered "I'm trying to get ready for my stepdaughter, Natalie, who is coming to visit this weekend, and I've been papering and painting and whatnot. I thought I'd take a break and go to Craftopia in Peoria. Would you like to tag along?"

"Sure!" answered Ashley. "We'll be back by dinner, though, right? Matt will be home from work, and these boys ... that is, Joe ... is always starving."

"I can get us home by dinner," I answered, and Ashley nodded.

"Be right there. I'll grab my purse."

She reappeared a moment later and we walked outside together. Out of the corner of my eye, I saw Cole and another boy heading off in the other direction. Ashley followed my gaze, and shook her head.

"Cole and my Joe. Kids had a half day today so now they're hanging out together. Best friends. Cole's got six brothers and sisters, and his family has a very small home. He spends most of his time with us. He wants a room of his own, I suppose—or sort of his own. He shares with Joe." She glanced at me.

"I think you mentioned Cole's family when we first met," I commented. "They're the ones that live on the next block?"

"Yes, that's it," answered Ashley. "They're good kids. Just need somewhere to be." Ashley smiled.

I opened the door to my garage and climbed in the Prius, and soon we were pulling in the parking lot at Craftopia. We spent a pleasant hour browsing the shelves and chatting about some of my projects. I found a set of artificial birds in a variety of different colors, so I bought those and began considering what sort of branch I might use to hang across the picture window. I had cardinals and blue jays and goldfinches. They would be pretty all lined up in the window. I bought a few sprigs of artificial greenery as well. Ashley found some Christmas ornament kits and some tie-dye tint on sale, plus a basket and some spray paint. She was happy and animated when we climbed back in the car to head home.

"We went to get things for you, and I ended up buying out the store!" she announced, putting her bags in the back seat.

I laughed. "But I got what I wanted. These birds are going to be perfect. My stepdaughter's coming on Friday night. Maybe we can put them up while she's here, if we don't get too busy."

"That'll be fun." Ashley watched the landscape streaming by the car window. "Any word on your basement?"

"What about it?" I asked. "Oh, you mean the padlock thing. No, nothing. I think all that excitement's over."

"Good," said Ashley. "Hey, what did you think of Brad Stanton?"

"Brad Stanton? From the sheriff's department? Ashley, I swear you must know the whole universe."

Ashley laughed. "Well, not the whole universe, but I do know him. Isn't he amazingly good looking? And you know, he was at the Abbott house when it was robbed."

"Abbott?" I drew a blank for a moment. "Oh, you mean the estate sale where the paintings were stolen?"

"That's the one," said Ashley.

Chapter Eight

"Really?" I queried. "Not the off-duty cop who chased the thief on foot?"

"Yup," said Ashley.

"He did mention the robbery when he came to my house after the break-in."

"Yeah? What did he say?" Ashley was back to gazing out the window.

"Oh, just that there had been a robbery in the area and they'd keep an eye out. I've been wondering about that."

"About what?"

"About the robbery."

"Oh." Ashley looked at me and smiled. "What was your question?"

"Well, you said the thief took off across the field and his friend left in a car. I'm wondering how he ran all that way through a bunch of corn and then hid while carrying a painting."

Ashley nodded. "Well, it wasn't paintings they were after. He didn't leave with any artwork. They went to steal jewelry."

I nodded. "That explains a few things. Do we know what the other guy stole? The one who got away?"

"No one knows for sure." Ashley sent me a sideways glance. "Probably nothing. But …"

I grinned. "You do know something."

Ashley grinned back. "Well, Matthew's brother's neighbor works at the sheriff's department, and the news sort of got back to us."

"Your brother-in-law's neighbor told you?"

"Well, no," said Ashley. "He told Matthew's brother, who told Matthew, and Matthew told me." She giggled.

"And you're going to tell me, right? Seems only fair."

"Naturally!" Ashley exclaimed.

I settled back in my seat, wishing the drive from Peoria to Burtonville were a little longer. I had the feeling this was going to be an interesting story.

"Here's the skinny," said Ashley. "The two thieves went to the house together. One pretended to be interested in the art and began asking Mrs. Abbott a bunch of questions. She couldn't stop talking about this painting and that painting, and while she was occupied the other guy wandered off and went to her room, opened her safe and emptied it. Except Brad ..."

"That's Brad Stanton, from the sheriff's department?" I interrupted.

"Right. Brad was there—off-duty—doing some shopping of his own. He likes art, and I imagine he thought maybe he'd buy a couple of pieces. He caught sight of the robber going upstairs and followed him. Caught him in the act."

"How'd the thief get in the safe? And how'd he know there was jewelry in there?"

"That's the awful part. Turns out he was related to Mrs. Abbott, which was why she wasn't really paying much attention to him and what he did. She kept talking to his friend. He was a second cousin or something, named Marcus—I can't remember his last name."

"Someone in her family was the one who robbed her?" I frowned and felt a stab of fierce anger. I despise schemes to rob or dupe the elderly. Having the perp be a relation was even worse.

"Apparently," answered Ashley. "I dunno how he got in the safe, except that it seems as if neither of them were particularly nice guys, you know? I doubt her safe was a super-secure one anyhow. But to get back to the story ..."

"Go ahead." I turned the car onto Beale Street. "Darn it. We're back already. Do you want to come in for a minute?"

Ashley looked at her watch. "Sure. It's only 5:00. My hungry men won't be all clustered in the kitchen for another forty-five minutes."

I laughed. I pulled the car in the garage, and Ashley and I unloaded our packages.

"I'll help you carry those home. Just leave them by the door." I let Rowdy outside, then invited Ashley into the kitchen. "C'mon in here. At least I've got a place to sit! Living room furniture comes tomorrow."

Ashley pointed at the walls. "Your wallpaper looks real, real pretty. I wish I could do something like that."

"I'll come over and help you sometime," I offered, and Ashley smiled at me.

"Thanks!"

I pulled out kitchen chairs and we sat down. "Back to the story?"

"Yes, the story. So Brad caught Marcus stealing the jewelry, and he was bringing him downstairs when his friend caught sight of them and gave Mrs. Abbott a shove right at Brad. In all the confusion, Marcus took off across the cornfield, and his friend jumped in his car and drove away. Brad was super mad that he let them get away, and as soon as he was sure Mrs. Abbott was okay, he called for help and then took off after Marcus."

"And they looked and looked for him."

"That they did," said Ashley. "They looked everywhere, walking down the rows of corn, and they had had dogs and everything. But they didn't find him until all of a sudden he ran across your yard, talking on his cell phone."

"Calling his friend to pick him up, I'm guessing?" I asked.

"That was earlier," said Ashley.

"What?"

"That was earlier. What happened was he was on the phone to the sheriff's office. He told them he'd called his friend, but his friend hadn't answered his phone or tried to call him back, and since he double-crossed Marcus and left him behind, Marcus would tell the authorities who his friend was as a sort of deal or barter or something. And he'd give the jewelry back. He was cussing and swearing something awful. He'd left a voicemail for his friend, threatening to tell. The message also said he'd written down who his friend was and where he lived and the names of everyone in his family, and he was turning it over unless his friend came to get him. But he didn't come, so Marcus called the sheriff."

"Did his friend ever come?"

"Nope. And no one knows if Marcus had a change of heart after he called the sheriff or what happened, because he ran into the road, and Madeline Burton hit him with her car. Not purposefully, of course. But she and Burt had another argument and she was mad, and speeding, and he wasn't looking, I guess, and she ..."

"Yes," I said hurriedly.

"And," Ashley went on, "Marcus got hit before he told the whole story to the sheriff. He didn't tell his friend's name, and he didn't say where he'd left the stuff he'd written down—only that the sheriff would want to pick up his friend because his friend was on parole."

"Seems like he said quite a lot before he got killed," I commented.

"Yeah, but he left out the important stuff. Matt's brother's neighbor said they would've gotten more information out of him if he hadn't been so mad and swearing. Probably that's why he didn't see Madeline coming."

"Probably," I echoed. "Wow." I sat for a minute, staring out the front window. "So basically, Mrs. Abbott's whatever-he-was ... cousin?—went to her house with a friend, and he stole jewelry and his friend maybe stole something, or maybe not, and the friend got away and Marcus got killed before he could turn his friend in."

"Yup, that sums it," said Ashley.

"Too bad they couldn't have found out who Marcus's friend was before Marcus got hit."

"Yeah," agreed Ashley. "He was being kind of cagey about it. They think he was going to deal and see if he could not be charged. I guess he doesn't have to worry about that anymore. Since he's dead, that is."

"Right," I said. "Did Mrs. Abbott at least get her jewelry back?"

"She will eventually, I suppose. It might be evidence or something. I'm not sure."

"It's a sad story," I said. "I feel really sorry for her. Not only getting robbed, but by someone related to her, and then having him killed on top of that."

"Yes," said Ashley. "She closed down her sale after the robbery, and her kids came and helped her lock up the house. Now she's living in a little place near them. There's a bunch of that going around here. We've got a lot of elderly people in Burtonville. People who've lived here for ages. Now all the houses are getting sold and new people are moving in. People who don't know the community."

I glanced out the window.

"Oh," Ashley went on hurriedly. "I don't mean you. That is, I *do* mean people like you, but you're really nice and I can tell you'll fit in here, and …" She hesitated, looking confused and embarrassed.

"I knew what you meant." I smiled at Ashley. "I look forward to getting to know the people in

Burtonville. Maybe I'll have a little yard party or something before the weather turns cold."

"That'd be nice. You'll like everyone here. People here have problems—like people everywhere. Like the Burtons. Like Cole's family. But we take care of each other."

"Of course," I said.

"I better get on home." Ashley looked a bit flustered. "Get my men their dinner. This has been fun," she added. "Did you mean it about helping me with wallpaper?"

"For sure. And you should stop by this weekend. Natalie will want to meet you."

"Okay!" said Ashley, beaming. I helped her gather up her bags and we walked together down Beale Street toward her pretty yellow house and her waiting family.

Chapter Nine

"Halloooo!" Natalie hurried across the driveway, her face covered in smiles, a shopping bag and an overnight case over one arm and a big bouquet of mums in the other.

I ran to relieve her of her packages and gave her a hug. "Pull your car into the garage once we're unloaded."

"Okay," she answered, her eyes sparkling. "But first, flowers for you!"

"Thank you, honey! Just perfect for my kitchen." I opened the door and ushered her to the living room, where she paused to look around.

"Wow! This place sure has changed. I love the wallpaper, and your furniture, and there's Daddy's Grand Canyon photo and everything. You *have* been going nuts."

"Only a little bit," I said. "And not because of you coming, or not *only* because. I wanted to get things all settled, and I've got so many ideas! Wait 'til I tell you about it. I'll take these to the bedroom." I carried her suitcase and the shopping bag down the hall and set them on the bed.

Behind me, I heard her cry, "Rowdy! How's my main man?" When I walked out, she was sitting on the floor and Rowdy had his big head in her lap. She looked up at me, grinning. "He looks like a happy guy. He's all settled in. I can tell already."

I smiled. "He likes his yard."

"So, what's on the agenda?" Natalie asked. She stood up and swiped at a small spot of drool on her jeans.

"Dinner tonight with Louise," I answered. "Then tomorrow we can go exploring, or for a walk, or whatever you'd like. It's a cute village, and there's excellent pizza."

"Ah! Pizza!" Natalie grinned. "I can tell Burtonville and I are going to be great friends."

I put the chrysanthemums in a vase and set them on the counter. Then, after Natalie and I had a cup of coffee and exchanged news, we moved her car and began bustling around the kitchen, putting shrimp and peppers and onions on skewers, tossing a spinach salad and firing up the grill. Rowdy wandered outside to watch while we barbecued, and soon I saw Louise's red Taurus coming down Beale Street. She pulled into the driveway and ran to hug Natalie.

She held up a bottle of wine. "I brought Moscato and lava cake makings for dessert," Louise exclaimed and, "Hey, Rowdy!" as my dog came lumbering around the garage. "I swear, Marianne, he looks more like a bear every day."

"A teddy bear," crooned Natalie, scratching him on his head. "Bring the food in. The shish-kebobs are nearly ready, and there's salad and everything!"

Louise walked inside, exclaiming over the house and admiring my living room. "It's beautiful," she pronounced. "So *you,* Marianne!"

Soon we were settled in the kitchen and eating voraciously. I sighed contentedly as I piled shrimp and veggies on my plate. I was spending the evening with my two favorite women in all the world. I beamed at Louise, beautiful with her blonde hair pinned up in a gold clip and one tanned shoulder peeking out of an asymmetrical sweater. I beamed at my beautiful stepdaughter, who was feeding Rowdy bites of bread, and at Rowdy, who was taking the treats so gently in his huge jaws.

Still beaming, I went out to the living room to pull the drapes, and I tried to keep beaming when I spied that dratted gray sedan creep by again. Craning my neck, I attempted to see who was at the wheel, but the car moved out of sight and I couldn't make out anything but the outline of the driver's shoulders. I did, however, catch the license plate number and I ran to jot it down before I re-entered the kitchen.

Natalie, in her way, immediately caught my change in mood. "What's the matter?" she asked, tossing a shrimp tail in the bowl on the table.

Louise, who was standing at the stove melting chocolate, glanced over her shoulder.

"What? Is something wrong? What's the matter with who?" she asked ungrammatically, blowing a strand of her blonde hair out of her eyes.

I frowned. "It's nothing. Or nothing much. I've been trying to get myself acclimatized to being here, I guess. And getting over a couple of weird things."

Louise turned all the way around. "What weird things?"

"Don't burn the chocolate!" Natalie and I said simultaneously.

Louise giggled and turned back to the stove. "Okay, lava cake first, weird things second. But talk while I cook. What is it?"

"Nothing, I think. Just a string of coincidences and a creepy thing or two."

"Creepy?" Louise added eggs and flour to the chocolate and poured the mixture in custard cups. "Hang on a minute, you guys. Let me finish this and then I can really listen."

Natalie and I exchanged glances and grinned. We three were equals in chocolate addiction, and lava cake was a staple in our get-togethers. Louise put the custard cups in the oven, set the timer, and then came to the table.

"So, what's creepy?" she asked, looking first at me and then at Natalie.

"Creepy's probably the wrong word," I began, and Natalie interrupted.

"We'll make our own conclusions about descriptors. Tell."

And so I did. I told of the basement and the lock and the no-lock, and the noise in the night, the robber in the cornfield—or possibly not in the cornfield. And the gray sedan parked across the street that kept returning—or at least I thought it was the same sedan. As I related the story, I thought I sounded paranoid even to myself.

"Wait," said Louise. "This sounds like the Case of the Mysterious Basement! Ooh, Marianne! I can be Bess and Natalie can be George."

"Who's George?" queried Natalie.

"Who's George?" exclaimed Louise, appalled. "Girl, you need to spend more time reading good literature and less time with your nose in The Manual of Psychopathology."

"But I'm a psych major!" Natalie protested. "I'm supposed to be reading The Manual of Psychopathology! Are you contributing to the delinquency of a graduate student?"

"Ladies!" I interrupted their banter. "No bickering. We must be mannerly! Natalie, Louise is referring to Nancy Drew mysteries. You know, the three friends? The series of books?"

"Ah, Nancy Drew," said Natalie. "Now I know what you're talking about. Never read any of the books, though."

"You're hopeless," laughed Louise.

"Never mind," I comforted Natalie. "I'll loan you one of my old copies. You can expand your intellect."

"When I'm on winter break. Right now I'm busy with psychopathology."

"Fascinating." Louise rolled her eyes.

"It *is* fascinating! All about the social, genetic and biological causes of mental disorders. We're looking at this study where—"

"Don't get her started," I said to Louise. "Or else you're going to be tempted to counter with Diogenes or Antiphon or someone, and no one wants to talk tragic literature at a party."

"Too true," replied Louse, "And we need to get going on the mystery. I lost track of the padlock. It seems to appear and disappear like magic."

"No kidding."

Louise was right. That padlock was like a specter, coming and going at will.

"We need a timeline!" crowed Natalie. "When's the lava cake going to be out of the oven?"

Louise glanced at her watch. "Five minutes."

"Okay!" Natalie pushed her chair away from the table, sending it skidding across the linoleum. "I'll be right back! I'm getting my computer!"

I rescued the chair, then got up to fetch forks and napkins.

Soon my stepdaughter had bustled back to the kitchen carrying her laptop, and Louise set custard cups full of sweet, chocolatey, hot lava cake on the table. "Hang on," said Natalie. "I gotta put my keyboard skin on. That chocolate could put a serious dent in my term paper." She affixed the silicone cover and set her laptop aside. "Now hand me some lava cake so I can get my brain working!"

Louise slid a custard cup in her direction. "Have at it, woman. Feed your head."

Then all was silent as we dug in to the hot, chocolatey goodness, and once again I felt my worries start to slide away. A string of coincidences. Wasn't that what it all was? Little things, stoked by moving in craziness and anxiety over Duffy—who still hadn't phoned me—all piling up to become something they weren't.

"Okay." Natalie licked her spoon and then the edge of the custard cup where a little chocolate still lingered. "Let's get started. I'm powering up my spreadsheet program … annnndd … here we go.

What's first?" She looked from me to Louise and back again.

"What's first?" I echoed. "Well," I thought back to *Fibber McGee*'s and Louise and going to get the padlock. "When I got to the house, I had to get a lock for—"

"Before that …" interrupted Louise. "You told me there was supposed to be a lock on the door when you moved in, and there wasn't."

"Right. Okay." I thought for a minute. "It all started, I think, when I spied this little house on Beale Street. I said to myself, 'That's the house for me,' and I contacted the realtor, and we walked through."

Natalie's fingers began clicking on her keys.

Chapter Ten

Half an hour later, I was finished, as were six custard cups of lava cake. Louise sat back in her chair and patted her stomach. "Why did I eat so much? It was the good company and the fascinating story. I kept going and going."

"Ugh," I agreed. "I did not need that second dessert."

"I did," said Natalie. "I'm on student rations usually. So here's what I've got so far. Mummy visits the house and likes it. Realtor puts a padlock on the basement door because it just seems like a good idea. Her nephew comes and takes it off for some reason. We aren't sure why. Mummy buys a new lock and puts it on, there's a noise in the night and *Poof!* padlock is gone again. Mummy gets a third lock and it stays on. In the meantime, a car begins casing her house."

"I'm not sure about the casing part," I put in quickly.

"*Maybe* begins casing her house," Natalie amended.

Louise narrowed her eyes. "Where in there did the robbery happen?"

Natalie looked at me. "That's right, we need to add that. I know the date because I looked it up on the Internet. Was the lock on or off?"

I pondered that. "I'm not sure. But I don't think it's related."

"Why?" said Louise. "Didn't your neighbor say the thief might have been hiding in the basement?"

"Well, yes. She did say that, but I'm not sure how likely it is."

"We're including everything, even if unlikely," pronounced Natalie. "I've got the robbery date and I've put it on the timeline. We can call the realtor and find out when she put the lock on and took it off."

"Okay. And if we're including things that might or might not be related, the cable company guy showed up at one point and for a minute I thought he was trying to get into the basement," I said.

"Lock on or off?"

"Off."

"Aha." Natalie's fingers clicked on the keys of her computer. "And when did you see the gray car?"

"Which gray car?"

"There are *two* gray cars?!" Louise exclaimed.

"I'm not sure. I saw a gray car parked across the road one night …"

"Lock on or off?" Natalie queried again. "I'm adding that as a field in my spreadsheet."

I frowned, thinking. "Off. I went afterward and got the first new lock."

"What about the second car?" asked Louise.

"I'm not sure if there is one."

"What?" Natalie looked at me, her brow wrinkled.

"I don't know the model of the car I saw parked. It was sort of nondescript, you know? Then a gray car has driven past several different times, but …"

"Lock on or off?"

I hesitated, thinking. Then, "On," I said. "At least usually, especially after I got the second lock. The first lock I bought was probably on for a few hours, then gone for another twelve or so, until I got the new lock. But I'm not sure it's the same car, anyway."

"Marianne, you can't be Nancy Drew if you don't notice models of cars!" Louise exclaimed.

"I got the license plate number tonight."

Louise and Natalie exchanged satisfied glances. "Nancy Drew, she is," Louise said solemnly.

Natalie pushed back from the table and studied her computer screen. "Want to know what I gather from all this?" she asked. "I think the robber *was* in your basement, and I think he *did* hide something down there. Your neighbor ... Amy, was it?"

"Ashley," I corrected.

"Right, Ashley." Natalie added that to the spreadsheet. "Ashley told you he'd stolen jewels. I'm guessing he left a bag of jewelry down in the basement and the second robber wants it."

"Down there?" I shook my head. "It's a pit. Or maybe not a pit, but a mess. Piles of stuff everywhere."

"What better place than that to hide something?" Louise asked.

"Well, that's not very comforting," I said. "And I realized I left something out. Ashley said there was a man here. She startled him and he ran away."

"When was that?" Natalie stared at me. "Lock on or off?"

"Before I moved in, but not much before. And the lock was on, she said. She saw him try to open the basement door."

"What was she doing here?"

"Bringing cookies. She's sort of the neighborhood welcome wagon."

"I'm adding her to my list of suspects." Natalie tapped on her keyboard.

"Oh, no, I don't think so," I said. "She's just … she's just a neighbor. I don't think she would be involved in a robbery or anything."

"Nonetheless," Natalie said darkly.

"I think Natalie's right," Louise commented. "If we're going to be sleuths, we shouldn't leave anyone out."

I shrugged. Ashley didn't suit my no-doubt-stereotypical notion of a jewelry thief. "And what about this unidentified man?"

"I added him, too." Natalie looked up from her typing. "We leave no stone unturned, no clue unexplored."

That made me laugh aloud. "So what's next, Bess and George?"

Natalie grinned. "Tomorrow we three are searching the basement. Right, Louise, er, Bess?"

"Yuck. You guys don't want to mess with the basement while you're here. We're having fun, and that won't be fun."

"Yes, we do want to do it," responded Natalie instantly. "And we're finding that missing photo, too."

"What missing photo?" asked Louise, piling dishes in the sink.

"She lost her photo of her and Daddy in San Diego."

"Oh, Marianne!" Louise exclaimed and gave me a sympathetic look. "You must be so sad! How did it happen?"

"Truthfully, I think it may have gotten thrown out." I felt the familiar tug in my chest. "I tossed so much stuff when I got here. Piles and piles. And I still have more. There's stuff in the bedroom waiting for a dumpster."

"Well, for Heaven's sake, don't toss anything else 'til we can go through it," said Louise. She turned on the warm water and squirted soap in the sink.

"You don't need to wash the dishes." I sounded feeble even to myself, and Louise—predictably—ignored me.

"Everything will come clear soon," said Natalie. "We'll find the hidden booty in the basement, and your photo is just tucked away somewhere."

"Right." Louise nodded and began stacking plates carefully in the rack. "Don't worry anymore. We'll find everything tomorrow. Marianne, I'm so glad you kept this Blue Willow."

"So am I. And who is the 'we' that's going to find everything?"

Louise looked over her shoulder. "Nancy, Bess and George, right? Now we've got two mysteries to sleuth out. The Case of the Mysterious Basement, and The Case of the Lost Photograph."

Suddenly I was beaming again. I had *such* good friends, and no one could have a better daughter. Rowdy groaned and turned over in his place by the door, so I beamed at him, too.

Louise, who had been looking over her shoulder, laughed. "Marianne, you look so contented, it's positively disgusting."

"So where're we going to put everyone?" Natalie asked. "Slumber party, right? So we can get going early tomorrow?"

"I'll do the couch," offered Louise. "Now I can claim to be the first person who slept on it. Can I borrow a toothbrush? And some jammies?"

"Anything you want." I laughed.

Natalie helped me carry a pillow and blankets out to the living room and make a sleeping spot for Louise. "This is going to be fun," she said. "Sort of like old times when we used to get together and watch movies. Before I started grad school."

"You're right," I said. "We can do a movie tonight, too. Let's push these blankets off to the side for a bit. Popcorn?"

"Well, yeah!" Natalie grinned.

"We're doing a movie," I announced to Louise, going back to the kitchen and pulling out a pan.

"I just washed that!" Louise protested.

"It's for popcorn."

"Girl, you need a dishwasher."

"No, I don't," I countered. "Where would I put one, anyhow?"

"Good point." Louise set the last custard cup in the drainer and wiped her hands on a dishtowel.

"Hey! 'Rear Window' is available on pay-per-view." Natalie called. "Seems appropriate, right?"

"I'll get the popcorn going," I said. I grabbed three bowls and put the popcorn on the stove. As the last few kernels were popping, I turned off the burner, divided the popcorn among the bowls and joined Natalie on the couch.

Louise walked over to the picture window and pulled back the drape. "Just getting in to character." She grinned at us and peered outside. "I gotta make sure … Hey!"

Natalie and I swiveled our heads to look at her. Louise let the drape drop closed.

"There's a gray car out there."

Natalie and I leapt off the couch, and I rescued the popcorn bowl at the last minute, setting it safely on the end table. We crowded in next to Louise and she pulled the curtain back a fraction of an inch. In the gloom, we could see a car parked under a tree down the road. A gray sedan that looked awfully, awfully familiar. In the dim light from the street lamps, I could see the vague outline of a figure behind the wheel.

Natalie looked at me soberly. "Let's call 9-1-1."

"Because of a parked car? C'mon, I don't want to become public enemy number one for the sheriff's department when I haven't even lived here a month," I protested.

"But, Marianne, this is seriously scary," said Louise. "What is it doing there?"

"It's parking," I answered. "Who knows why? And we don't even know if it's the same car. It's facing the wrong way to see the plate. And it isn't in front of the house or anything."

"It's a Buick Regal," commented Louise. "Is that the same car you saw before?"

I shrugged. "It's hard to tell. It sort of looks like it."

"Maybe we should sneak out and check the license plate!" Natalie started for the door.

"No!" I exploded. "What if it's an ax murderer?"

"An ax murderer?" Louise raised her eyebrows.

"Okay, not an ax murderer, but I don't want us creeping around. What if we get caught? What if whoever-it-is doesn't appreciate us looking at their car?"

Natalie went back to the couch and sat down. "Maybe we better just watch the movie. No one's going to break in with all of us here and the lights on and everything. Mummy's probably right. We can't call the sheriff 'til we have proof. We'll know more tomorrow. We're going to look in every possible nook and cranny of that basement."

"I think that's the place to start." I sat down next to my stepdaughter and threw a comforter over our legs, then held it back for Louise to join us.

Natalie started the movie and we helped ourselves to popcorn. It really was almost like old times. All except for the part where I kept feeling that frisson of anxiety. I glanced over at Natalie and saw her rubbing her arms as if she felt cold, except I knew she wasn't.

Chapter Eleven

We awakened to a fall morning with a vague nip in the air, reminding me that winter was coming and if I planned to get any of my outside projects done, I'd better get busy. Because of the chill, Natalie proposed that we begin our day indoors with an all-out hunt for the missing photograph, and move outside to attack the basement once the sun was higher in the sky. We decided to carry all the basement items to the yard, since I presumed most of it would be thrown out anyway, and I didn't want to sideline the progress I'd made in organizing indoors. I brewed two pots of coffee and a vat of oatmeal, and after we had fortified ourselves and Louise took Rowdy for a walk down Beale Street (I remembered to warn her about the Paulsens) we began the search.

"I didn't see the gray car," Louise commented when she returned to the house, hanging Rowdy's leash on its hook. "I wonder what time it left last night."

"I looked outside around 2AM and it was gone," said Natalie. "I'm glad. Maybe you're right and it's nothing, but it gave me the creeps anyhow."

Louise made a face. "Me too, but let's not get distracted. We gotta find the picture."

So we pulled out every unpacked box and bag we could find, even the recent purchases from Craftopia, and went through them carefully. Once we had finished that and found nothing, we searched in drawers and behind furniture, then went to the garage.

"I'm checking your car trunk," called Louise, and Natalie grunted as she hauled a box down off the work bench.

"I've already looked in that box," I said. "It's tools and a few cans of spray paint."

"We might as well be thorough," answered Natalie, pulling back the cardboard flaps.

But the photo was nowhere to be found, and we all agreed we'd looked everywhere we could think of—even in the bottom of the trash can. The only conclusion I could draw was that, somehow, in the rush and bustle and confusion of the move and all the throwing away, I had tossed the precious package into the recycling. For a moment, I felt tears lurking behind my eyes, but Louise put her arm through mine and led me back up to the house and

Natalie's cheerful: "Never mind, Mummy. I am positive I can make you another copy!" brightened my outlook a little, although I did throw in a stubborn, "I liked the one I had," which made Louise pat my arm.

"Would you like to make another trip to Craftopia next week to look for a nice frame?"

"Maybe," I answered. "Let's have some lunch. Are you guys sure you want to tackle the basement this afternoon? Somehow I'm getting out of the mood."

"And miss finding a 40 carat diamond or something hidden down there?" Louise asked.

"Or a three foot rope of pearls?" put in Natalie. "Or a tiara?"

I grimaced. "I'm telling you, there's nothing in that basement but cobwebs and piles of trash. I haven't set foot in it since I've been living here, except when the sheriff's office came. No one has, and why would we? It's like a health hazard."

"Pshaw, we scoff at health hazards," said Louise. "What's for lunch?"

Pleasantly stuffed with grilled cheese sandwiches and tomato soup, we went back outside and I unlocked the padlock.

"How come you don't use the lock on the knob?" asked Louise.

"Because I don't have a key, and at first this seemed easier." I frowned. "I'd like to get a key made for it and keep the knob. It's unusual, don't you think?"

"Look at all the engraving," Natalie said. "I bet it's an antique."

"That's what I thought. I'll get someone to make a key. It's on the list."

"Okay, look out, basement!" exclaimed Louise, and we descended the stairs.

Attacking the basement was just as arduous a task as I expected it to be, and perhaps worse. The wooden shelving units were piled high with crates and boxes, scrap lumber had been stacked in the corners, a wide shelf held dusty cans of paint, and there was a workbench covered with a tangled mess of wire, old gloves, rusted tools, yellowed newspapers, heaps of envelopes, carpenter's pencils and all manner of other rubble that collects, despite our best efforts, as the years pass by. Looking around, I resolved to not let the space get that way again.

"There's a lot here, but it's not really that bad," Natalie announced. "Not that dirty at all. Just cluttered and stuffed full of things."

"I think we should pull it all out in the yard," announced Louise. "Why not? Then on Monday you can call for a big dumpster and what you don't want you can get rid of."

"I agree," said Natalie. "Let's do it."

I fetched three pairs of work gloves, and we pulled things up the stairs to spread out in the yard. We organized them by 'Definitely Pitch,' 'Possibly Pitch,' 'Needs Fixing' and 'Definitely Save.' The 'Definitely Pitch' pile was divided into a pile for recycling and a pile that could be donated, and as a last resort, discarded. We took breaks for coffee and then for soda, as the air warmed and it was now a beautiful day. Soon the basement began to empty, but, as I expected, there was no sign of anything of much value—and certainly nothing like a string of pearls or a diamond. Clusters of Burtonville residents wandered by as we worked, and a few stood and watched, calling out encouragement or condolences. A man—Brian Paulsen, I discovered— offered to help cart some of the trash away. He spied Rowdy crashed under his tree and didn't turn a hair, and I wondered if Ashley Midden had exaggerated the Paulsens' hatred of dogs. Ashley herself stood in the driveway for a few minutes, a curious expression on her face.

I introduced her to Natalie and Louise.

"Finding anything good?" Ashley asked. "Wish I could help, but I promised Matt …"

"No problem," I said. "This is probably a three-woman job anyhow. We'd just get in each other's way."

"Look at all you've moved out! What are you finding?" she repeated.

"Oh, this and that," I answered vaguely. "A lot of stuff I still need to sort through."

"Ah," said Ashley. It looked as if she would have liked to say more, but a brown pickup truck pulled up and Ashley looked over her shoulder. "Here's Matt. I'd better go." I waved at her, and she climbed into the truck with her husband.

"Do you have a tarp?" called Louise. "We can throw it over this stuff and leave it out here to deal with tomorrow if we run out of time today. Especially the stuff you want to donate and get rid of. No point in carting it back downstairs."

"I think I saw one on the workbench." I went down to look, leaving Louise and Natalie out on the lawn bickering over a picnic basket and whether it belonged in the 'Possibly Pitch' or 'Needs Fixing' pile.

"It's definitely got possibilities," I heard Louise say, and Natalie answered, "The handle's coming loose. It isn't worth it," and Louise countered with, "You can't find baskets like this anymore. I'll ask her if I can have it if she decides to pitch it."

I lifted the tarp, but as I did so, under it I spied a familiar box. Snatching it up, I pulled back the flaps and there it was—my precious photo—wrapped safely in the quilting. "Well, well, well," I said aloud. "Wouldn't you know? There's treasure in this here basement, after all." I gazed at the box thoughtfully, turning it over in my hands, and I had the feeling a mystery had been solved, or at least I'd discovered a significant clue. The Case of the Unreasonably Angry Duffy.

I glanced up as Louise came down the stairs. "What did you say?"

"Look what I just found!" I pointed at the box. "Stuffed under the tarp."

Louise put her hands on her hips. "What is it? Not that photo!"

"In living color," I answered, pulling it out and holding it up. "All safe and sound."

"How in the world did it get down here?"

I hesitated. Should I throw Duffy under the bus? Did he deserve it? Probably. But could I do it? Would I do it? No. I'd deal with Duffy later, but I was so grateful to have my picture back that I decided to take the rap. "This is embarrassing—" I began.

"You brought it down here yourself, didn't you?" Louise interrupted, putting her hands on her hips. "And forgot? Good thing you're my best friend forever."

I was spared having to answer by what happened next.

"Natalie!" called Louise. "Your mom just found the missing photo! Let's get this tarp out." She reached and gave the tarp a hard yank. There was a creak and a crack, and the wooden shelving unit began to tip.

"Look out!" I yelled, pulling her out of the way as the shelves over the workbench tore loose from the wall and hit the next ones, toppling the entire thing onto the basement floor in a jumble of broken wood and dust.

"Well!" exclaimed Louise, her voice shaking slightly. "Thanks, Marianne. That could've given me a bit of a headache if it had landed on me."

Natalie came pounding down the stairs. "What happened?"

"Shelves broke," said Louise shortly. "But we're fine. Marianne, I'm sorry. What a mess! I didn't realize that was going to fall over."

"It's okay. I'd rather replace the shelves anyway. I'm just glad they didn't fall on you!"

"Um, yeah. Me too. But I feel badly I broke them."

"Don't worry about it, Louise. The wood was probably old. And it gives me an excuse for a trip to the hardware store."

"Like you need another of those."

"It's okay," I insisted. "I could never have accomplished all this without you guys helping, and we've done a huge amount of work."

Louise looked around. "Yeah, I guess this is pretty much done. I was thinking we could bring some of the 'Definitely Save' stuff back down, but …"

"No, enough for today," I pronounced. "I can finish this up alone, and buy some good sturdy shelving before I move anything back. Maybe some big tubs, too."

"But …" protested Louise.

"No, enough," I flapped my hand at the room. "There's hardly anything left to clean out, and we're all tired. And we accomplished one of our goals. We've got the missing photo. I'll come down tomorrow and move the broken shelves to the trash."

"We found the photo?" Natalie squeaked.

I opened my mouth, but Natalie immediately jumped to the same conclusion Louise had and gave me a peck on the cheek. "Never mind, Mummy. It doesn't matter. At least you've got it."

We extracted the tarp from the mess on the floor, carried it out to the yard, spread it over the 'Definitely Save' and 'Needs Fixing' piles, and I stuffed all the papers we'd found in a box to sort and recycle. "Let's get a pizza," I said. "You guys need to experience Burtonville's best."

"We didn't find my tiara," Natalie commented.

"I'll get you one for your birthday." Louise patted her shoulder.

"A really cool one with a big diamond?"

"You got it, girl."

"Well, okay then." Natalie grinned.

"I need a shower before we go out in public," Louise said.

"Me too." Natalie made a face. "Yuck."

"Right," I agreed. "I don't want to scare any of my new neighbors. You and Natalie duke it out over first dibs. Just save me some hot water."

I left the two of them arguing, "You go … no, you go … no, you go … no, you go," laughed, and went into the kitchen to feed Rowdy.

Chapter Twelve

Soon the three of us, newly showered and smelling like my favorite peach shampoo, were striding down the road arm in arm, with Rowdy in the lead. It hadn't taken him long to figure out that Leonard's meant a hamburger for him, and he was hot on the trail.

"God, this is fun," said Louise. "Just like old times! Remember when we used to sit up until nearly dawn playing Gin at your old house, Marianne?"

"We could have a game tonight," I offered. "Want to spend the night again?"

"I better not. I've got tons to do to get ready for work on Monday, and if we sit up 'til dawn, I'll be doomed."

"Maybe one game over pizza?" asked Natalie.

"Okay, one game," Louise agreed. "But don't let me lose track of the time. I've got too much work."

"Nose to the grindstone," commented Natalie.

"'...to be idle is to become a stranger unto the seasons,'" I quoted Gibran, and then felt a twinge. *Damn it, Duffy.*

We ordered our pizza and stood by while it was in the oven, inhaling the delicious aroma of melting cheese and crisp, parmesan crust. Rowdy made urgent whining, slurping noises at Natalie, who held the hamburger bag.

"Patience, Rowdy!" Louise gave him a pat. "Marianne, did you actually feed your dog?"

"Of course not. I just pretended to," I answered, and Louise grinned.

When the pizza was ready, we carried it home and spread out plates, napkins and playing cards on the kitchen table. Soon we were all busily munching and playing an energetic game of Gin, except Rowdy, of course, who fell sound asleep in the corner after devouring his hamburger. We played another game. And another. And another. Natalie won two; I won one; Louise won one.

"Okay, you guys, this is it," Louise said, dealing cards. "'Revenge is sweet and not fattening.'"

"Is that from one of your tragic poets?" Natalie demanded.

Louise laughed. "No, Hitchcock. It seemed fitting for this weekend's adventures."

Rowdy lifted his head and stared around at the door, licked his chops and went back to sleep.

"What's got him so worked up?" remarked Natalie, and I shrugged. "Maybe he's dreaming of hamburgers."

Louise gazed at Rowdy. "That constitutes worked up? I swear, Marianne. Half the time no one would even know you owned a dog. He doesn't bark; he just lies around all the time. Are you sure he's a dog?"

"Aw, Rowdy!" exclaimed Natalie, and bent to scratch his head. Rowdy snored on.

I glanced out the window. "I hate to say this, Louise, but I feel forced to point out that it's pretty late and you wanted to get home."

"Oh, my." Louise stretched, groaned and pushed back from the table. "I better get a move on." She stood up and walked to the living room. "I'll get my stuff gathered up, but first let's—" She didn't finish her sentence.

"What …?" began Natalie.

"Hush!" Louise whispered loudly.

Natalie and I stood up, but Louise came hurtling back into the kitchen. "You guys, there is someone out there!"

"Out where?" I started towards the living room.

Louise grabbed the back of my shirt. "Out in the back yard! Looking under the tarps!"

Natalie pushed past us and went to the window, staying well back so she could peek out without being seen from the yard. Louise and I crowded up behind her. What I saw made my breath catch in my throat. A dark figure was bent over one of the piles of items we had lugged up from the basement, sorting through it slowly and methodically, pushing things aside, digging in a heap of old rags and straightening to lift an occasional object up to the moonlight.

"Who is it?" Natalie whispered, tugging on my sleeve.

"I have no idea. Whoever it is, he or she is wearing a parka and a hat. And it's too dark to tell if I know them."

"Let's turn on the outside light!" exclaimed Louise.

"No!" I said. "I'm calling 9-1-1. Maybe they can catch them in the act."

"Coming all the way from Prairie City?" Natalie protested. "They'll never get here in time. Is the door locked?"

Louise glanced over. "Yes."

"Maybe they'll turn around," said Natalie. "So we can see better." She and Louise huddled shoulder to shoulder, staring out the darkened window, while I found my cell phone and called 9-1-1 dispatch.

"It doesn't look as if they're stealing anything," whispered Louise. "Just looking for now."

"If they find that tiara, I'm going to be furious." Natalie gave a nervous laugh. Louise put her arm across Natalie's shoulders.

I felt close to tears. Two visits by the sheriff's department in under a week? My dream house was turning into a nightmare. The dispatcher advised us to stay in the house with the doors locked, and under no circumstances to go out in the yard. A trooper was on the way and we were not to hang up the phone. I held my cell phone to my ear and joined Natalie and Louise again at the window. The figure had moved to the far pile, but still had its back to us.

"Don't they know we're here?" Natalie whispered.

"Maybe they don't care. Or maybe they figured we're asleep," said Louise. "I don't like this."

"Me neither," I said. The bump in the night culminating in the missing padlock had given me no desire to confront anyone in my yard. In fact, I was feeling decidedly frightened. *What's next*, I thought, *a hit man?*

"Is the intruder still there?" the dispatcher asked.

"Yes," I answered. "Wait, he might be leaving. Yes, he ran around the garage and I can't see him anymore. How far away is the cruiser?"

"It'll be there very shortly, ma'am. Do not go outside. Keep the door locked and stay out of sight."

"We are." I looked out the window again. "But I think it might be too late. I can't see him anymore."

"The officers are nearly there."

"This is horrible," said Natalie. "I think he sneaked away. Now we'll never know who it is or what he was doing."

"I think Nancy Drew would have gone out in the yard to investigate," added Louise.

"Louise, that isn't funny!" cried my stepdaughter.

"No, it isn't. I'm sorry, sweetheart. I wasn't really implying anyone should go outside. I'm scared and making stupid jokes."

I squeezed Natalie's shoulder and then Louise's. "At least they're gone."

"But what did they want?" wailed Natalie. "Mummy, I don't think you should stay here! Someone breaks into your basement and now this?"

Secretly, I was wondering if I agreed with her, but suddenly a spurt of anger shot through me so strongly that my hands began to shake. "No one, *no one* is driving me out of my house! There was nothing down in that basement but a bunch of trash, and if I have to make that point to whomever it is who thinks something different, then I'll pile everything up tomorrow and torch it—right out in plain view. If they are watching, they can just give up and stop harassing me. I'm sick of this."

"What if there's something valuable?" Natalie asked timidly.

"There. Is. Nothing. But. Trash," I repeated loudly, and Louise patted my arm.

"I do agree with you, Marianne. The bonfire might be a bit of overkill, but still. Call Monday, get a dumpster, and get the stuff gone. If there's nothing in the basement, then no one can want anything."

Moments later, two sheriff's cruisers pulled up in front of the house, and the dispatcher signed off. I saw several officers climb out of the vehicles and begin walking around the yard, flashlights shining. They checked the piles of things from the basement, circled the garage, and walked the perimeter of the house. Finally I saw a figure approach the front door, and I opened it to admit Officer Stanton, who, I thought glumly, must have been wondering if the sheriff should open up a station in Burtonville to deal with my problems. I saw Louise's eyes widen when she spied him. The man *was* good looking. Tall, dark and handsome was a descriptor that fit him very, very well.

"Hello again." He smiled at me. "What happened?"

Stumbling over our words, and occasionally talking over each other, we explained what we had seen.

"We took a look around the yard," said the officer. "There's no one there now. What's in the piles? Anything someone would want to steal?"

Natalie glanced at me and I shook my head stubbornly. "It's mainly old tools, cloths, dried up paint, broken furniture. You saw the basement before we cleaned it out. It was organized well enough, but a collection of years of stuff. Old and pretty much worthless in my mind. I was going to recycle or scrap most of it."

"Is everything you brought up from the basement out in the yard?"

"I brought some boxes of papers inside to sort in case there are house records," I said. "Mainly old stuff; lots of it very yellowed. And there are a few items still down there I intend to keep, but not too much."

"Do you have a yard light?" asked Officer Stanton.

"Yes." I turned it on, and he joined the other officers outside, again walking around the garage and the house, and shining a big flashlight behind the tree and out into the cornfield. He opened the side door of the garage and disappeared inside for a few minutes.

"That is the best looking man I've ever seen," Louise breathed. "He looks like a cross between George Clooney and John Cusack. And those eyes!"

I smiled at her. "Yes, and I'm well on the way to being on a first-name basis with him," I answered. "All I need to do is keep having break-ins and we could get to be besties."

"He can be my bestie any old time." Louise controlled her expression when he knocked again and I opened the door.

"There's no one out there now," said Officer Stanton. "You saw him go around the garage and back out toward the street?"

"Yes." Louise nodded. "Hurrying, I'd say."

"Running, in fact," Natalie put in.

"Running?" Officer Stanton noted that on his pad. "Was he carrying anything?"

"Not that I saw," I answered. "If he took anything, it was something small."

"You said 'he.' Are you sure the intruder was a male?"

"No, actually I'm not," I said. "It was dark and we didn't want to turn on the light. Maybe we should have."

"You did the right thing," he responded. "Everything appears to be fine outside. Could've been a trash picker or a neighborhood kid or something, but there's been a lot of activity around here lately, and no one should be in your back yard. Keep your doors locked and be alert. Call us if you have any more trouble, or feel threatened, or see anything suspicious."

I frowned. "Okay."

Officer Stanton finished his notes, left a card with telephone information for the station, and went back out to his car. After a few moments, both the cruisers had driven away.

I glanced at my watch. "It's awfully late. Sure you don't want to spend the night again, Louise?"

"I better not. Although if the intruder comes back, maybe we could call the sheriff again." She waggled her eyebrows.

I smiled, but I was feeling very low. "You're welcome to stay if you like, but I know you wanted to get home. Go get your work done, and I'll call you tomorrow. It's been a wonderful weekend. Just really wonderful. Let's do it again. Without all the drama next time."

Louise gathered up her purse and coat. "You guys be careful. Take care of my Main Girls."

"We will," I answered.

"Keep the door locked!" Louise called over her shoulder as she went out to her Taurus.

"We will," I repeated. "I'll keep the light on 'til you're in your car and pulling out."

"Thanks."

Natalie and I stood at the living room window and watched until Louise's car was out of sight, then

I shut off the yard light and turned to look at my stepdaughter. "C'mon, kiddo. Let's hit the hay. You need to head out tomorrow, and there's no point in us being up all night fussing."

"Oh, Mummy." Natalie looked close to tears.

"I know," I said soothingly. "But we're all right. Maybe it really was a trash-picker or a kid. They shouldn't have been in the back yard. Not fun, but not threatening either. It'll be okay."

Natalie nodded, and we walked back to our bedrooms. *I probably wouldn't have called the sheriff's department had it not been for the basement break-in,* I told myself. *But could the two incidents possibly be related?*

I frowned, changed into my pajamas, and turned the bed covers back. But a moment later, I returned to the living room and double-checked that the dead bolt was securely fastened. Then I rested my hand against the door for a moment. "Go away," I whispered. "Leave us alone."

Chapter Thirteen

I slept restlessly, torn between wondering if my recent adventures were a tempest in a teapot, and being unnerved by the idea of people creeping around my home, even though nothing had been taken and no one threatened me. At least, not so far. I resolved to put a chair under the door knob on the door leading to the basement from inside the house, notwithstanding the outside lock. I would wait until Natalie left, however. She was too upset already.

Natalie and I met in the kitchen at the coffeepot, both of us looking groggy and heavy-eyed. She joined me at the table, hands folded around her mug.

"I suppose I don't need to ask how you slept?" I said.

"Not too well. I'm real hesitant to leave today, Mummy. What if something happens?"

"Well, nothing's really 'happened,' has it?" I answered reasonably. "We think someone was in the basement, but if they were, they're gone and haven't been back so far as we know."

"What about the person in the yard?"

"I expect it was someone different." I patted her hand. "Or maybe it was the same person, but we don't have any reason to think they want to hurt anyone. It seems as if they are looking for something. Who knows? Maybe they found it last night. They took off running."

"Probably because they realized we were watching," Natalie said darkly. "I wish this would go away. Do you think the sheriff's department will really keep an extra eye out?"

"Yes, I do," I answered, hoping I was right.

Natalie and I whiled away the morning in a pleasant way. Natalie exclaimed over the birds I bought at Craftopia, and we did some coloring in one of her favorite adult coloring books. Soon, both of our moods had lightened considerably, and after we took Rowdy for a long walk through Burtonville, Natalie reluctantly put her suitcase in her car and stood with me at the picture window looking out at Beale Street.

"This really is a nice house in a nice town. I feel badly you're off to a bumpy start."

"Things'll sort out," I answered. "By the next time you visit we'll have nothing to do but indulge ourselves."

Natalie grinned. "I can't come next weekend, but maybe the weekend after. I'll let you know. And you better call me if anything, and I mean *anything,* happens!"

"Like when I feed Rowdy or something?" When Rowdy heard his name, he flicked one ear.

"You know what I mean."

"Yes, I do. I'm sorry. If anything worrisome happens, I will let you know right away."

"Okay then." Natalie gave me a hard hug, climbed in her car and backed it out of the garage. At the street, she opened the window and leaned out. "Call me!"

"I promise!" I waved, and watched as she drove away.

When she was out of sight, I went back in my house and looked around, feeling somewhat at loose ends. I spied the photo of Duane and me where I had left it the previous afternoon, and I debated phoning Duffy, but then decided against it. *What were you thinking?* I asked him silently. *What did you think I was thinking?* I carried the package to the den, slid the scrap of quilt under my laptop on the desk and set the photograph in its place of honor on the corner. When that was done, I stood for a long time staring out the window, thinking.

I was roused from my reverie by a knock on the front door, and when I made my way out to the living room, I was surprised to see Ashley Midden waiting on the step, her face pink and her eyes puffy from crying.

"Ashley!" I stepped aside to let her in. "Is everything okay?" I didn't even bother trying to pretend I hadn't noticed the telltale marks of her weeping. She looked perfectly miserable.

"Oh, Marianne!" she burst out, and started crying again, mopping at her face with her sleeve.

I handed her a box of tissues. "What in the world is wrong?" I asked. "Let me fetch you a cool washcloth to put on your cheeks. That always makes me feel better."

"No!" she cried, and I stopped in my tracks, turning back to face her. "I have to tell you something. I wish I didn't have to, but I do. I'm afraid you're going to absolutely hate me, but it isn't my fault, really. Matthew says it is, but it really isn't. I didn't know what to do, and I thought maybe if we just … if we just didn't …" She sputtered to a pause, swiping at her eyes with a frayed tissue and sniffling noisily.

"Maybe you better tell me what's going on," I said gently. "I'm not sure what's happened."

Ashley gazed at me with bloodshot eyes. "You're going to be so upset."

"Just tell me."

"Okay. This is about your basement."

Naturally, I thought, and frowned. *The bloody basement.* Ashley looked at me apprehensively. "Go ahead," I said. "Don't mind me. I've had a rather unpleasant couple of days."

Ashley dropped her face into her hands. "I didn't mean for this to happen!"

"Ashley!" I exclaimed. "What. Is. Wrong?"

"Well," she sniffled. "You know Cole? Cole, Joe's friend?"

"Yes."

"Well, I told you he didn't have any space of his own, and this house was empty for so long, and the basement … You know, it wasn't locked and no one lived here, and it's quiet and really pretty comfortable down there. Maybe not for you and me, but for a kid who wants a place to play video games and do what kids do. Didn't you have a fort when you were a kid?"

"Of course," I replied. "All kids have forts."

"Cole began hanging out down there. Took a sleeping bag and an old chair and I don't know what-all. I'm positive, *certain,* he didn't damage or harm anything. He just messed with his phone and he and Joe played some games and talked, and they even camped down there one night. Or maybe more than one night. Okay, they did it several nights, but I assure you, they are good boys! They didn't hurt anything or do anything. I know they were trespassing, but ..."

I tried not to sound as aghast as I felt. "So it's Cole and Joe that have been messing around in the basement?"

"No! Well, sort of. Sometimes. Here's what happened. Cole and Joe didn't realize you were moving in. That is, I told them, but you know—kids. Cole had some stuff down there and I told him he absolutely had to get it out because how was he going to explain being in your basement without permission. Then the realtor locked the basement up and they couldn't go down, but when we realized the lock was gone, one night after you moved in but had gone out, Joe went to help Cole get his stuff. He was down there when suddenly here came the cable guy, so Joe stayed in the basement real quiet, thinking when he'd gone he'd get the rest of the things and sneak out. But then you put the lock on and he was trapped. Cole came running to our house in a panic, and we had to do something to get Joe out, right?"

"Right," I said, and thought, *I don't suppose it occurred to you to come and tell me all this a little sooner?*

"So you can see what we did?"

"What did you do?"

"We got Matthew's bolt cutters and sneaked back and I let Joe out. Then we ran home. But still we weren't sure if everything was gone, that is,

119

whether there might be still some of Cole's or Joe's things left behind. So last night ..." Ashley began really sobbing this time, her shoulders shaking and her face buried in her tissue. I handed her a fresh one.

"What happened last night?" I urged. "You came back, didn't you?"

"Yes! I wanted to take a look in the piles to make absolutely sure. You know, to make sure nothing was there that would show that Cole and Joe were in your basement, where they should *not* have been. I wish I'd never let them do it, but it seemed harmless. No one lived here, and they're good boys! They're just kids!"

"It really frightened us, seeing you out there." I tried to speak mildly, despite my annoyance. "We thought it was a robber. And that night when Joe was locked in, it scared me. I didn't know what was going on."

"I'm so sorry! Matt's furious, and I'm afraid he'll not want Cole to come over anymore, and then Joe'll be so upset. I had to come over and tell you before anything got any worse. You called the *sheriff*!"

"Well, yes." I said. "Wouldn't you have?"

Ashley gulped. "You didn't know when we cut the lock, it was only us trying to get Joe out. And looking for things that we own anyway."

I felt a twinge of irritation, but I stomped it down, and when it began to simmer again gave it a new stomp.

"And then you took me to Craftopia, and I thought we could be friends and everything. Now ..." She looked at me closely, and when I didn't answer, she blurted, "That's not all of it." I sighed, and Ashley rushed on. "You need to hear the end of the story. Last night, when I was looking at the stuff in your yard, a man showed up."

"Good," I said sarcastically. "Great. Who was it?"

"I don't know, Marianne! I really don't. But I think ... I think it might've been the same man who was here before."

"What man is that?" I asked acidly, thinking of the stream, nay, the *parade* of men—and women, too—who seemed to be making a beeline for my basement.

"The one I saw right before you moved in. The one that was trying to get in the basement door. He saw me and I turned around and saw him, and I was so shocked and scared I ran home!"

I sat up straighter. "Where did he go?"

"I'm not sure. I think he had a car parked out in the street and he drove away."

Chapter Fourteen

"A car parked out on the street?" My mind flew instantly to the gray sedan. "What kind of a car?"

"Some sort of a van. When I realized he wasn't chasing me, I turned around and looked. I don't think he wanted to be seen any more than I did, and he didn't know I would be there. When he realized I'd spotted him, he left. Maybe he thought I was you."

"Maybe. So there were two people bent on rifling through the things in my yard last night?" I remarked sarcastically.

"I think so." Ashley blew her nose and looked at me over the top of her tissue.

"And you didn't know the other person?"

"No! Like I told you, I'm pretty sure it was the same man who was here the day I first came with cookies, but you hadn't moved in yet. I don't know who it was. He doesn't live in Burtonville. Of that I'm sure."

"What did he look like?"

"Like I told you before, he was sort of heavy and balding, although it was a little harder to tell his weight because he was wearing a thick coat like I was." Ashley sniffled. "I know pretty much everyone around here, and I didn't know him. Really! I'm telling the truth!"

"All right." I tried to soften my tone of voice. No one likes to be frightened, but no one likes to feel foolish, either, and I was definitely feeling that way. The awful intruder was Ashley? And Ashley's son? "The reason I ask about the vehicle," I said, "is that there's been a car out in the street. A couple times. Several times, in fact. I don't know if whoever it is might be casing my place or watching me, or what. It's really very uncomfortable."

"That's awful," responded Ashley instantly. "A van?"

"No. This is a gray sedan. A little older. I have the license plate number."

Ashley narrowed her eyes. "What kind of car did you say?"

"I didn't, but it's a Buick Regal."

Ashley started to smile. I, however, was still struggling to find anything humorous in the situation, and I had to fight to hold in my temper. Seeing the expression on my face, Ashley sobered quickly. "Bob Burton drives a Buick Regal. And he's often parked here and there along the streets. After he and Madeline have an argument, he leaves and drives around. You'll see him a lot. Not during the winter. During the winter, he goes in to Prairie City and hangs out at the truck stop."

"You have got to be kidding me!" I exploded. "The car I've been worrying about, and the man I was certain was casing my house, is my neighbor hiding out from his wife? I need a cup of coffee." I started toward the kitchen, stopped and looked over my shoulder. "You want one?"

"Um ... sure?" Ashley said hesitantly. "You won't put hemlock in it or anything, will you?"

At first, I wasn't sure what she was talking about. "What?" I snapped, and then. "Oh. Of course not. I wish you'd said something earlier about Joe and Cole. But no, I won't poison your coffee." *Wait 'til I tell Louise and Natalie,* I thought. *They won't believe this.* I hoped neither of *them* would want to poison Ashley's coffee.

Ashley followed me to the kitchen, stepping carefully over Rowdy, who was sprawled in the doorway. "I really am awfully sorry. For scaring you and for not trusting you. I was trying to protect the kids. And ... what about that man?"

I sighed. "Oh, I don't know, Ashley. I'm still trying to make sense of all this. Are you sure, absolutely sure, that he was coming into the yard, and that it isn't someone who lives here? It could've been a trash picker."

"Most trash pickers take stuff from the curbside, not from a back yard, and not stuff from under a tarp. At least, not usually," said Ashley promptly. "He's not from Burtonville, and I've seen him twice now at your house, doing stuff that seemed suspicious. Did you tell the sheriff?"

"No. And I'm still not going to. It's all just a little too random. And besides, what am I supposed to say to him? How about 'Ashley Midden, who was sneaking around in my yard uninvited, saw a man sneaking around in my yard uninvited?'"

Ashley looked downcast. "Yes, I see your point."

I poured two cups of coffee and turned around to look at her. She had such an unhappy expression on her face that I decided to give her a break. "Look." I held out one of the mugs. "Truce?"

"Truce?" Ashley stared at me, her eyes wide.

"I'll stop making comments about you being in my yard," *and about your son and his friend being in my basement*, I didn't say, "if you will talk to me in the future if anything like this happens again. Or if there are things I really ought to know," I added, since the idea of anything remotely similar ever happening again—*Really? Somehow I'd managed to lock Joe Midden in my basement?*—seemed so far-fetched that it didn't bear contemplating.

"Okay," Ashley said. "I promise."

"Truce then?"

"Truce," said Ashley.

And then somehow, despite everything that had happened, we managed to pass a reasonably pacific hour talking of other things. Ashley told me about the ornaments she was making from the items we bought at Craftopia, asked after my birds-in-the-branch project, and offered to help me carry things back down to the basement. "The weather's going to turn bad," she said. "Cold and rain for the next few days. Everything'll get wrecked."

"There's nothing much to wreck," I answered. "But before you leave, please sort out whatever belongs to Joe or Cole, or whatever else you want, and take it with you. There's just one pile—the one nearest the house—that I plan to keep for sure, and I'll bring those things in this afternoon. Everything else you can have. Some of it needs repairing," I added.

"All right."

Ashley threw a quick glance at my face. Apparently she didn't see anything alarming there, because she excused herself and I glimpsed her out the window taking a quick look under the tarps. Then she hurried away down the sidewalk without a backward glance. It didn't appear she had taken anything, but by then I cared so little about the piles in the yard that it wouldn't have mattered if she carted the whole mess away.

As I watched her leave, I realized another of my recent round of mysteries was solved. This one The Case of Why Ashley Left So Abruptly the Other Day. She was, of course, trying to cover for her kids. I sighed. I would be very glad not to think about the basement for a while. I was quite thoroughly sick of it.

Despite my antipathy toward all things basement, I knew I had to dispose of the stuff we'd carried out and piled in the yard. So I forced myself to move the 'Definitely Save' items into the garage. There were very few. An old sign that read 'Beale Street,' and was likely an antique; two salvageable hammers; the tarp, which was in surprisingly good condition; a nicely carved wooden box; two pairs of gardening gloves; and a carton of blue glass that I might turn into a wind chime or a garden ornament. I decided to relinquish the 'Needs Fixing' pile to the recycle bin. I really didn't want to fix anything else; I just wanted everything out of sight and out of mind. Soon, the yard was considerably more organized.

One final item I carried inside; a curious carved statue fashioned of some sort of metal—perhaps brass—that featured a vine winding up a tree trunk. Peeking out from the leaves were a variety of animals. Some I recognized and some I did not. The sculpture was old and quite heavy, and I wondered if it might be valuable. I set it on a shelf in the living room to clean up and examine more closely.

Once I was finished in the yard, I went down to the basement and lugged the broken shelving upstairs to the discard pile and swept the room. Then I surveyed the area, taking stock of the space and what I might store there. One good, sturdy set of shelves, I decided, and a couple of plastic tubs would do it. No point in cramming in more than I needed. Basements always had a way of collecting stuff, and I had no intention of giving in to that impulse. Satisfied, I went back inside, happy to be where it was warm. Ashley was right; we were in for a cold snap.

Rowdy opened one eye when I walked inside. "Hello, my man," I said. "Ready for some more sorting? We've still got papers to go through."

Rowdy closed his eye again and I sighed. I wasn't going to get any assistance from that quarter. Sometimes I thought Rowdy really should have been born a big rug rather than a dog. I toted the box of papers out to the kitchen table and began to sort them. The majority were old, yellowed, and with the ink so faded that they were mostly illegible, but some were records of home improvements, repairs and even construction notes for when the porch was added onto the house. There was a list of addresses and phone numbers that looked newer, along with some scrawled and indecipherable notes, a rather touching 'I Love You' card that looked as if it might have been penned by a small child, a packet of old telephone bills, a lumber receipt, and newspaper clippings from Peoria and the New Prairie Gazette that chronicled area happenings for the last thirty years. I set those aside and resolved to phone the historical society, if there was one, to see if there was any interest in preserving the articles in their collection.

Finally, I decided I had done all I could to dispose of the rubble from the basement. I put all the discarded papers in a bin and pushed them in the corner of the living room for recycling. Perhaps the next step was to go buy a set of shelves and work on getting them assembled until it was time for dinner.

Chapter Fifteen

I put the chair under the basement door knob. Despite Ashley's recent revelations, the basement had begun to feel ominous to me and I didn't like the sensation. Feeling irritable and uneasy, I gathered up my coat and hat, and headed out to my Prius. First stop would be the Burtonville Hardware, although I thought it was unlikely they would have the sort of shelves I was looking for. They didn't, although they had a display of vases decorated with grouted stained glass chips and I bought one for Natalie. I debated whether to go to Peoria to the big box store, or to try Prairie City first, and I settled on Prairie City. Putting my carefully-wrapped vase on the floor in the back seat, I headed out.

Prairie City was a cute town, larger than Burtonville, but with a small-town look and feel, a vintage downtown and several restaurants that looked fun to visit. The hardware store was at the end of Main Street, with a large, convenient parking lot into which I pulled and parked my car. Inside I found widgets and doodads and home improvement gizmos that made my heart sing, along with several different sets of shelves and shelving systems that would be perfect in my basement.

While I was contemplating the glories of one of those beauties, and rethinking what I might do with my basement space, someone walked by in the aisle across from me, paused and said, "Marianne Reed?"

I looked up. Across from me was a tall man with curling sable-colored hair and beautiful dark eyes. Tall, dark and handsome. None other than our local law enforcement, out of uniform and on a hardware run just as I was.

"Officer Stanton!" I reached across the display and shook hands with him.

He laughed. "Call me Brad. What brings you to Prairie City's humble hardware store?"

"Hardly humble!" I smiled. "There are many delights here. I'm on the hunt for some new shelves for my basement. Mine suffered a sad accident."

He frowned. "Not another incident?"

"No … well, no, not exactly," I added, trying to decide whether, in fact, there had been an incident or not. I decided *No* was the correct answer. "The problem was homemade shelves, old lumber and too much stuff stacked on it. We had a small breakage event. Now it's time to reorganize and set it all to rights. These units look as if they'll do the trick. What are you shopping for?"

"Trying to find some under-bed hampers." Brad Stanton frowned. "I live in a small apartment, and even with the few things I have, I'm finding it difficult to stow stuff." Then, "You said, 'Not exactly.' You didn't have another unwelcome visitor, did you?"

Could I explain without divulging Ashley's role? Did it matter if I didn't intend to press charges? At a minimum, it seemed it would damage her reputation if the word got around about what happened. People would talk, and she'd mentioned her husband was already angry. Really, there was nothing to tell, so I wouldn't.

"No more unwelcome visitors. And suffice it to say," I added mildly, "that things weren't quite as they seemed. It's all resolved now, and I think there'll be no further trouble."

"Well, good." Brad glanced around the shop. "Any chance you'd like to make your purchases and then go grab a bite? We've got pretty good restaurants for a small town."

I looked up at him, at his tanned face and rugged good looks, his kind eyes. And no significant other, apparently, if one could judge by the 'small apartment' remark. My treacherous heart flew to Duffy, who was still AWOL, and at whom and about whom I was still very angry and confused. I reeled my heart back in.

"Sure," I answered.

"American cuisine or Italian?"

"I had pizza last night, so let's go for American."

"You got it," said Brad.

We separated and he walked on through the store while I spent another ten minutes contemplating shelving choices. I finally settled on the shelving system, which had spaces for narrow and wide containers, seemed easy to assemble, and came with several bins with labelling options. I paid for it just as Brad strolled over.

"Need help getting that out to your car?"

"I think the store will help."

"Probably." Brad lifted the box onto his shoulder. "I got it, Pete!" he called to the cashier. He pointed his chin at the bins. "If you grab those, I'll take this."

I picked up the bins and we loaded everything into my Prius. Then he pointed down the street at a small restaurant with a bright blue canopy, sporting a sign that read, **The Eatery**. "That's it," he said. "Shall I meet you there? Park out in front. The back lot's probably full."

I laughed. "Dinner crowd already?"

"You'd be surprised. It's a popular spot."

I moved my car down the street, and walked inside the brightly lit café. Brad Stanton was already standing by a table near the window, and I joined him there, noticing that he smiled and nodded to several people sitting nearby, and they returned the greeting. We sat down and he handed me a menu. "Can't go wrong with pretty much anything, though I might avoid the clam chowder. I keep telling Mandy it's salty, but she says is supposed to be. Matter of taste, I guess!" He grinned.

"Okay, no clam chowder," I answered. "Maybe the bean soup and a Caesar salad."

"Good one. I usually have the turkey sandwich with mashed potatoes. Given how cold it's turned, I think that's my choice again today."

We ordered, and while we waited for our food to arrive, he asked me about my move to Burtonville and what made me leave Peoria. I offered my standard, "Because I wanted to," which was easy because it was true. I also told him about my secret garden and the Paulsens, who might or might not hate dogs and their 'defecations.' I told him about Natalie and about the big back yard for Rowdy, and I discovered he was remarkably easy to talk to— smiling at all the right points; serious at the serious places. All in all, a delightful companion, and the time passed quickly.

Finally, I got to the basement episodes, guided there, I thought, rather expertly by Brad Stanton's gentle questioning. I wondered at his curiosity, and decided to tell him just as much as he needed to know, without giving away Ashley's part in the story. The waiter brought our food, and I continued with the basement narrative, hoping to put it to rest once and for all.

"It turned out to be pretty much a misunderstanding," I said. "A neighbor had been given permission to use the area to store some of their own things ..." I deliberately avoided indicating if the neighbor was male or female. "... and when I moved in, they were a bit taken by surprise." Not entirely true, but close enough to the truth that it ought to ward off any uncomfortableness for Ashley—assuming anyone ever figured out it was she whose son had been in the basement to begin with.

"I get it," said Brad, and I thought he did, including the part where I had deliberately avoided mentioning any names.

He put his chin on his hand and looked out the window, poking at the turkey gravy with his fork. The silence lengthened. I finished the last bites of my soup and set the bowl aside, then looked across at him. He frowned, and I was a bit taken aback, wondering if he was angry that I hadn't been more forthcoming.

"Marianne," he said at last. "I'm in a bit of a difficult position, but I've decided I need to share something with you."

"Oh?" I put my hands in my lap and wondered where on earth he was going with his comment.

"This has to do with the robbery in Burtonville. You know, at Olivia Abbott's place?"

"Of course."

"I don't know how much you know about the players in all that."

"I know that Mrs. Abbott had a relative that was involved, Marcus-something, who got hit by a car, and that there was another person who got away."

"Yes," said Brad. "We're pretty much convinced we know who else was involved in the robbery besides Marcus Probst. His brother, Kenny Probst, is also implicated, but we're quite sure he wasn't at the Abbott place when the robbery went down. He and Marcus hobnobbed with another man, a bad actor named Zachary Kestor. Kestor's out on parole. He has a pretty long rap sheet, including burglary and assault. He's got an alibi for the time of the robbery." Brad's voice trailed off and his frown grew.

"And?" I prompted.

"And," Brad went on, "before he got killed, Marcus told us he wrote down the names and contact numbers of people who would swear Kestor was with him at Olivia Abbott's. Probst was furious at Kestor for hanging him out to dry when they took off from the Abbott place, and wanted to trade the information for leniency."

"I kind of know most of this," I commented.

"How's that?"

"I probably better keep my mouth shut," I said. "I suppose someone was sharing facts that should have been kept confidential."

"Small towns." Brad shrugged. "Information flies everywhere, and no one keeps anything very secret for very long."

I nodded.

"Anyway," Brad went on. "What you probably don't know is that the word on the street is that Probst threatened Kestor that he'd turn the document over to the sheriff and Kestor wants that paper. If he's involved in a robbery, he's going to go back to jail for a very long time."

"Oh." Suddenly my stomach didn't feel very good.

"And my problem," said Brad, "is that I think that paper is still out there somewhere. I think Probst ditched it before he got hit and killed, and Kestor knows that. I can't prove it—that's just what I think. I think Probst hid it and Kestor knows where—or approximately where—and he's going to go after it."

"Oh," I said again. Alarm quivered down my arms.

Brad looked at me, and now his frown was replaced by worry. "I'm sharing details with you that are part of an ongoing investigation, but I like you, Marianne, and I'm not happy about the trouble you've been having. I'm concerned about your safety. I know you said it was a misunderstanding, and I know you are deliberately not telling me a lot."

I felt myself beginning to blush, and I tried to cover it by dabbing at my lips with my napkin.

"I want to be sure you'll be careful. Maybe I'm blowing this out of proportion—certainly some of the others at the station think I am. Chalk it up to my gypsy ancestors." Brad chuckled. "But I've got a bad feeling in my gut about Kestor. And unfortunately, when I get a bad feeling, I've found it's usually a good idea to pay attention."

Chapter Sixteen

"Are you specifically warning me?" I asked.

"Just be careful," Brad answered. "It's easy to get lulled into thinking everyone's cozy and neighborly in a small town, and it isn't always the case. I liked you the first time I met you, and I'm hoping maybe you'll agree that we might grab a meal together again sometime. But, even if I didn't feel the way I do, I'd still be uneasy about all the activity around your house, in light of what I know."

"My neighbor saw a man in my yard," I said in a small voice. I guessed it was time to stop protecting Ashley and tell the rest of the story, although I'd still try to leave her out of it. "Someone she didn't know."

"Saw a man?" Brad looked vaguely alarmed. "Doing what?"

"She saw him twice," I answered. "Once before I moved in, trying to get into my basement, and then once when … once the other night, out in my yard."

"Why didn't you call me?"

"I did call you," I answered defensively. "You came to the house."

"You couldn't describe who you'd seen, though. Just that whoever it was seemed to be searching through the things on the lawn."

"Well, I found out about the man later," I said, and trailed off. "It's a bit complicated."

Brad stared at me.

"Well, it is!" I protested. "And the complicated part really isn't the important part. The important part is my neighbor saw the same man twice at my house. Someone who didn't belong there. Once trying to get into the basement, and then again the other night."

"Wasn't your basement locked?"

"Oh, not again!" I exclaimed. "That lock! In short, the basement was supposed to be locked, then it wasn't and then it was, then wasn't, and now it is again."

Brad looked confused.

"Never mind. It's a long story, and I actually want to call the realtor to clarify something about the lock situation when the office opens tomorrow."

"Why?"

"That's complicated, too," I said. "My daughter and my friend, Louise, and I were trying to figure something out; that is, we were trying to figure out the timing of when the locks were on and off compared to when the break-in occurred."

Brad sighed.

I dropped my face in my hands, shook my head and began to laugh. "I know this doesn't seem very funny to you, but from my perspective, it sort of is. At least the parts that aren't scary are a bit funny. Or maybe the whole thing is so incredible that it seems funny when I try to explain it all." I looked up at my dinner companion. "I wouldn't blame you if you were getting pretty angry right now."

"I'm not angry."

"Thank you. That's very forbearing. Do you think you could forget about my neighbor and my daughter and my friend, and maybe even about the lock? I don't think any of it is really relevant, except possibly the part where the realtor put the lock on— and then took it back off."

"Okay, I'll take your word for it." Brad shook his head. "But, my advice remains. Please keep an eye out. And call if you notice anything else unusual. Something doesn't make sense here."

I sighed. "I agree with you. In fact, that's why my daughter and my friend and I spent time talking about it. My neighbor thinks Marcus Probst was hiding in my basement after the Abbott robbery. You probably have heard that theory."

"I've heard it," said Brad. "There's no real evidence that's true—except now you've had two attempted break-ins. Did your neighbor—I presume we're referring to Ashley Midden, right?—say what the man she saw looked like?"

So much for protecting Ashley. "She noticed he was heavy set and balding. That's all I know."

"That's not Zach Kestor." Brad stated flatly. "Kestor's thin as a scarecrow and has a full head of hair. Could be Kenny Probst, but I'm not sure what he'd be doing hanging around. I may follow up with Ashley. See if she can give me some more details."

And I'll call her when I get home, I thought. If the sheriff's office started asking her questions, she would think I turned her in for trespassing, and it would scare her to death. I looked down at my watch. "I suppose I better get a move on. I need to get these shelves unloaded and turn in for the evening. This was fun, though."

Brad stood up from the table and picked up the bill.

"Let me get mine," I said quickly.

"You sure?"

"Positive."

"Okay, then. I meant it when I said I hoped I could see you again. And not as a sheriff's officer visiting a frightened woman, but as a friend who likes a good meal. I know some fine eating places the other side of Burtonville I could introduce you to."

"I'd like that." We paid our tabs and went out to the car. The wind had come up, and I covered my ears with my hands. "Thanks again," I said loudly. "I'm not going to linger. One of us will freeze!"

"Okay, see you soon. And pick up the phone if anything is making you anxious."

"I will." I climbed in the Prius, and soon I was motoring down the road back to Burtonville, gripping the wheel tightly as the wind tried to buffet my little car. I was grateful to turn into the driveway of the house on Beale Street, roll my car in the garage and bustle inside, leaving the weather behind me.

As soon as I was settled, I sat down at the kitchen table and picked up my cell phone.

"What?!" Louise shouted. "You went to dinner with that … that Adonis from the sheriff department? I'm completely and totally jealous!"

"It was a nice dinner," I admitted. "I really did enjoy it. But, it has a bad part. And I need to go back to the beginning of the story. The part where Ashley—"

"Do we have to?" Louise interrupted. "I'd rather talk about Brad Stanton."

"Well, going back to the beginning explains some things."

"Oh, all right. Go ahead."

And so I told her about Ashley's visit and about her son and Cole, and after Louise had finished expressing astonishment about the culprit behind the Bump In The Basement, fear about who the mysterious man might be, and another round of wishing she'd stayed longer in Burtonville so she could have been with me when I ran into Brad, she hung up and I phoned Natalie.

Natalie paid no attention to the dinner with Officer Stanton, but was alarmed at the story of what really happened the night we saw the figure going through the basement items in the yard. She immediately insisted that I come stay with her for a while, or else she would come stay with me. I managed to allay some of her fears, not without some difficulty.

"We have to remember," I said soothingly, "that this mysterious person may not be anyone threatening, or even anyone connected to the robbery and Marcus Probst. It might be someone entirely different."

"I still don't like it," Natalie answered. "Can you at least get an alarm or something? This is not making me happy."

"I'll look into an alarm," I said. "And tomorrow I'll call Loretta."

"And you'll call me as soon as you've talked to her," Natalie added instantly.

"Yes, I will call you, and you can round out your spreadsheet."

"I don't care about my spreadsheet. I just liked it a lot better when the person in the yard was a trash picker. I don't like it that it was Ashley, and I like it even less that there was someone else out there."

"He might still be a trash picker," I pointed out reasonably. "But at least part of the mystery is solved. And Ashley's no one to be frightened of."

"Only part of the mystery," Natalie grumbled. "And now there's a whole new wrinkle."

"I'm being careful," I said. "The sheriff's department is keeping an eye out. I'm sorry to upset you, but I promised to bring you up to date. Bess and George, right?"

"Bess and George," agreed Natalie. "I'm glad you called. But, let me know what's going on, would you? Please?"

"I will!" I exclaimed. "I agreed I would, remember?"

"Okay." She clicked off after one more, *"Call me,"* to which I sighed and responded, "I just did, Natalie!"

The next person I phoned was Ashley. I warned her that the sheriff might contact her for details about the man she'd seen in my yard, and reassured her that I hadn't mentioned Joe. Once she realized her secret was safe, she became very eager to be part of the questioning and vowed to do her best to remember as many details about my unwanted visitor as she could.

Finally, I set my phone down and went to the den to check my email and do some online searching for a knights-on-horseback wallpaper border. I was tired of basements and robbers and padlocks and phoning people, and even of the sheriff's department. It was high time I got back to what was close to my heart—my house. But, while I was online, and because of my promise to Natalie, I visited several websites and scoped out alarm systems. Soon I was lost in the wonders of the Internet, and I had found several more things to look into, including a raised garden system for my secret garden and some information on super hardy chrysanthemums that were guaranteed to bloom in colder climates. Perhaps the next batch I planted would stay alive in my flower beds after all.

Outside, it began to sleet.

Chapter Seventeen

I slept remarkably well under the circumstances, awakening with a renewed sense of purpose and with the goal of getting the den completely painted by the end of the day. After fortifying myself with two cups of coffee and an English muffin, I pulled out the fawn paint I had chosen for the room, found brushes and rollers and my step stool, Rowdy-proofed the door and set to it. By early afternoon, I was finished with everything except the ceiling, and I stopped to take a break, wiping my hands on a damp towel and feeling enormously pleased with myself. The room looked 100% better, and would be charming with Natalie's photos hung back on the wall and some pretty, new curtains. I decided the window dressing needed to be something cheery—maybe a soft green.

I went out to the kitchen for a late lunch and stared out the window at the slate colored sky. The weather had certainly turned bad awfully quickly. Going anywhere didn't seem appealing. Even Rowdy hesitated before heading outside to do his business. I gave him a little push and he finally walked into the wet, cold grass. I let him back in a few minutes later and dodged while he shook the rain off his fur. He went to the kitchen to lie back down, and I stared after him, pondering what to do next. I realized I still needed to call Loretta, and I'd been putting it off, so I resolved to get that out of the way before deciding any further how to spend my day.

I took my phone to the living room, sat down in one of the chairs near the picture window and made the call. Loretta answered right away, and after some obligatory small talk, I asked my question.

"Loretta, do you happen to remember when your nephew took the realtor key box off my door and took away the basement lock?"

There was a pause on the other end of the line, and Loretta asked cautiously, "Are you having a problem of some sort?"

"Not at all," I lied. "It's sort of a game with a couple of friends. You know, sleuths? Nancy Drew?"

Loretta laughed. "Oh! Nancy Drew. I used to read her endlessly. Hang on a sec. I think Jason's still here." The ubiquitous canned music started up and I sat back to wait. Another call came in and I sent it to voicemail, glanced idly at the screen of my phone. The call was from Duffy.

I nearly hung up on Loretta, then reminded myself that I was still pretty angry at Duffy, and kept on holding. I watched to see if he left a voice message, but nothing came through. Finally, Loretta returned. "Sorry for the wait. Jason was in the kitchen having a snack. Honestly, that kid."

"What did he say?" I prompted.

"He is pretty sure he picked the lock up the Tuesday after we closed. So that would've been about a week and a half before you moved in. That's pretty standard practice," she added, maybe a bit defensively.

So the lock was off when the robbery occurred, I thought.

"Hello?" came Loretta's voice.

"Sorry! I was thinking. Everything's okay. Thanks for the info." I was sure she thought my Nancy Drew tale was a bit thin, yet I didn't know how else to explain why I had phoned.

"You're welcome. Anything else I can do for you?"

I wanted to get to Duffy's call and see if he'd left a message, although there was still nothing showing on my voicemail. "No, not today. Hey, come by and say hello sometime. I've done a lot of work on the house."

"It's a deal," said Loretta, and we clicked off.

I checked my voicemail. Duffy had not left a message. Call him back or not? I needed to tell my co-sleuths, George and Bess, what I'd found out from Loretta, but they wouldn't be free from class and teaching until later and I didn't want to alarm either of them by calling in the middle of the day. I took a deep breath and phoned Duffy.

He answered immediately.

"You rang?" I said idly, and didn't say, *For God's sake, Duffy, after all this time?*

"Yes," he said. "Marianne, I have something to tell you." My heart began to slam. *He's got cancer or some horrible disease,* I thought. "I did something I'm not proud of," he went on.

Aha. My heart rate slowed. I was nearly sure I knew where this was heading, but the nasty side of me wanted to hear it out. "Oh?" I was pleased at how calm my voice sounded.

"Yes. You know that photo of you and Duane? The one you always had on your desk at the old place?"

"Um, yes."

"Well, I found it in the trash while I was helping you." I didn't respond, and he pressed on. "I retrieved it, and at first I thought maybe it had gotten in there by mistake. If I hadn't been so angry that you'd decided to move, I wouldn't have done what I did. It felt as if you had left me; as if you were discarding everything you had. And not just everything *you* had, but everything *we* had."

"I told you why I was moving, Duffy."

"Yes, but it never really made a lot of sense to me."

A flare of anger shot through me. "Well, that doesn't really matter, does it? It made sense to me," I said sharply.

He went doggedly on. "I thought you were trying to put some distance between us."

Was I? I wasn't sure.

"I was doing my best to not let it get to me, and trying to help you. I planted those flowers and helped you move boxes and recycle and all, yet I was really hurt. And then when I found that photo, it was sort of the last straw. I know you loved Duane, and that's okay. I didn't care that your house was full of your memories of him, even though he's been gone all these years. But when I saw you'd thrown out that photo, something in me sort of cracked. It made me feel as if you were throwing everything away, me along with it."

"Huh." I knew that was rather cruel, but I couldn't help it.

The silence stretched out. Finally Duffy said, "I took the photo out of the trash and I hid it."

"Really?"

"Yes. I put it down in your basement. I left it all wrapped up and everything, and it wasn't damaged."

"Why?" I asked.

"I don't really know. I've asked myself that over and over. You certainly had the right to discard it if you wanted to. But it made me so sad. It made me wonder if you were the person I thought you were. I was really, really angry."

"Did it occur to you that I might have been pretty upset that it was lost?"

"Later. Yes." There was another long silence. Finally Duffy went on. "You know how I feel about you, Marianne. How I've felt about you for years. It's easy to be wounded, I think, and to act in unreasonable ways, when there are strong emotions involved. Anyway, I wanted to let you know where it was in case you wanted it. And if you don't want it, that's fine. I know I was completely in the wrong. I'm not proud of behaving in such an infantile way."

"Duffy, you need to know that I found it."

"The photo? You did?"

"Yes, over the weekend when I cleaned the basement. That is, Louise and Natalie and I did."

"Oh," he said, and there was a short silence. I imagined him running his hands through his hair.

"I figured you had put it down there," I went on, "and I even thought I knew why. It turns out I was right. And *you* are right that I'm entitled to throw it away or not to throw it away. It's my property, my lost husband ..." To my horror, I thought my voice was going to begin to shake, and I paused for a moment. "My lost husband, and my decision to move to this house. Which I love, by the way. And which I hoped you would grow to enjoy, too. I never intended to discard my old life, and I'm not going to justify all that again. I explained it. I'm sorry you don't understand."

"Maybe I understand it a little better than I thought I did, or wanted to. But all that doesn't matter. I am deeply, deeply sorry, Marianne. For ignoring you and for pushing you away. For being out of touch. For everything. Really, that's all I called to say."

"Okay. Apology accepted. I kind of wish you'd asked me before deciding to go off and pout." I knew that was a low blow.

"Point taken. Yes, I was pouting. Yes, it was stupid and insensitive. I'm very ashamed."

"Okay," I said again. "I'm not sure where this leaves us."

"I'm not either."

"Well, if neither of us knows, perhaps the best thing is for both of us to do some thinking. Or some more thinking, maybe."

"I agree," said Duffy.

"Later then," I said, and only afterward realized that unconsciously I'd answered my own question.

Rowdy padded into the room and put his chin on my lap so I could scratch behind his ear, which I did, for a long, long time. Then I wiped a small—a very small—spot of drool off my pants, stood up and went into the den, Rowdy at my heels. I sat down in front of my computer, reached out with my right hand and touched the photograph. Touched it, very lightly, with the tip of my fingers.

Chapter Eighteen

Later I wondered what that gesture meant—the gentle brush of my fingers across that well-loved frame. Was it, 'Welcome home?' Was it a plea for advice or for forgiveness; for understanding? None of those answers were right, and perhaps I did it simply because I wanted to, I'm not sure. I recall sitting for quite a long time, while outside darkness began to creep across the cornfield, and rain started to fall again in cold, gray sheets.

I almost didn't hear the pounding on the door.

I peeked out the window and saw a tall man on the doorstep, hunched against the cold and looking soaked to the skin. While I watched, he pulled a cell phone out of his pocket, glared at the dark screen, and then put it away. He was lifting his hand to knock again when I unlocked the door and braced my foot against it to let it open only a few inches.

"Hi," I said though the gap.

He looked at me, drops of rain on his eyebrows and dewing his hair. His nose was red from cold. "Hello," he said. "I'm awfully sorry to bother you. Do you have a phone I can use? My car's dead, and so is this worthless thing." He held up his blank-faced cell phone. "I need to call my sister to come get me."

"Of course." I started to turn away. "You can use my ..."

I intended to hand him my phone through the partially-open door, but he threw himself forward and shoved it violently inward. The door hit my shoulder with such force that it nearly knocked me over, and then he was in my living room, panting slightly and pushing the door shut behind him. I managed to regain my balance at the last minute and opened my mouth to let out a yell, but he leaped forward, hooked an arm around my neck, held me against his body and clamped his hand over my mouth before I could utter a squeak.

"Don't scream!" he growled in my ear. "Do not scream. Do you hear me? Nod 'yes.'"

I nodded quickly, feeling bile rise in my throat and my pulse thundering in my ears. *Idiot! Idiot! Idiot!* I cursed myself. *It's easy to get lulled into thinking everyone's cozy and neighborly in a small town.* Hadn't I been warned?

The man eased his hand away from my mouth and I took a gasping breath, holding one fist to my stomach and dragging at the arm he had wrapped around my throat. My terror was making me feel light-headed, and for a moment I simply could not think. I inhaled, choked, inhaled again.

"I won't hurt you," said the man. "Not if you cooperate. I need help."

"What?" I croaked. "Help?"

"I need help," he repeated. "Help me and everything is going to turn out fine."

Even in my addled state I knew nothing was likely to turn out fine. If he'd needed help, why hadn't he simply asked, rather than forcing his way into my home and assaulting me? He loosened his hold a little more, while still preserving a tight grip on my arm, and kept me turned away from him. "I need something you have."

I didn't answer, but things were beginning to get slightly less muddled, and my brain stopped feeling as if it was moving in slow motion. "What is it?" My voice shook. At least I answered, though. That was something.

"A paper," he answered. "My brother left it here. In your basement."

His brother. Marcus Probst, the thief who might have hidden in my basement. Who apparently <u>*had*</u> *hidden in my basement after the robbery, after all.* Ashley's description of the man we thought might be Kenny Probst, the robber's brother, popped into my mind: 'Heavy set and balding.' This man was not Kenny Probst. He was lying. 'Thin as a scarecrow and has a full head of hair,' was how Brad Stanton had described the third man. Roger Kestor. No, Zach Kestor. I'd bet my knights-on-horseback wallpaper border—which I did not yet have—this man was he. The more dangerous of the threesome, on parole and with a long record. My brain was starting to function much better, although what good all that information was going to do me I could not imagine. What I needed to do was to get Zach Kestor, or whoever he was, out of my house. Play dumb. Perhaps that would help.

"Is the paper for your car?" I asked, and for a moment he hesitated. Then he gave me a jerk that nearly yanked my shoulder out of the socket. I moaned in pain. "Don't be stupid," he snapped.

So much for playing dumb. I cradled my shoulder in my other hand and stood for a moment with my head hanging, trying to fight down the pain and think again.

"I need the papers from your basement. The ones Marcus left down there."

He'd used Marcus's name. I knew from detective novels that wasn't a good sign. Anonymity was important to someone bent on mischief. My eyes flew to the chair propped against my basement door. Should I try to lure him down there? That seemed foolish, and I couldn't imagine what good it would do. My hesitation didn't help me. The man I was now sure was Kestor gave my arm another yank that made pain scream across the injured joint. I bent at the waist, retching.

"I cleaned the basement out," I gasped. "I don't know what paper you're talking about."

"It's got names on it. Maybe some phone numbers. I know you have it because we saw you and your friends emptying the basement. Nothing's been picked up yet. And your outside garbage can is empty."

A shiver ran up my spine. We'd been watched all the time we were carrying things up and down? And they'd been checking the trash cans? The thought was horrifying. *Louise,* I thought. *And my sweet Natalie.* What if they had chosen to make their move while the three of us were here together, or while we were outside working? *Too public,* I thought. *Someone in this cozy, neighborly little community would have seen them. And better to act with just one person to subdue. Or perhaps Kenny Probst wasn't keen on the idea of attacking a woman and Kestor had to go it alone.* All the papers from the basement were here, or most of them, anyway, in the sack not five feet away. If I gave him what he wanted, would he leave?

My ruminations were cut short when he gave my arm another twitch. "We're going to go get the papers from the basement and you're going to go through them. All of them. When we find the one I'm looking for, you're going to give it to me."

And then what? I thought. He'd revealed who he was, or at least enough about him and his cronies that it wouldn't be safe for them to simply go into

159

hiding. But, if he pulled on my injured arm again I was afraid I was going to faint, and I needed to stay alert.

"Over there," I gasped, pointing at the sack. "Nothing's in the trash," I added defiantly. "It's all being recycled." Stupid remark, but under the circumstances it was the best I could come up with. And—interestingly—somehow it felt as if a little bit of the power in the room shifted back to me. I stared at the bag, and at the other item I'd brought up from the basement—the brass carving sitting on the shelf. There had been that lined piece of paper with the addresses. Could that be the one he wanted?

"Get it," said Kestor shortly, pointing at the paper sack. He didn't let go of my arm, but loosened his grip enough for me to bend and pull the bag toward us. The warm press of his body made me shudder, and I hastily stood up again, wondering once more if I might gag.

"Dump it."

I tipped the sack over, spilling papers out over the floor. "There's one," I said breathlessly, "that had some phone numbers ..."

Kestor leaned around me and stirred the pile with his toe. "Where? Find it."

I balked. I couldn't bear the notion of stooping down again with him holding onto me. I twisted toward him, and that was when I saw it. Out of the den came a big, black dog that looked a bit like a bear, or perhaps a bit more than a bit, padding silently on huge soft feet. Rowdy, who never barked. Rowdy, who was more like a fur rug than a dog, and who had been lying close by when the knock came on the door. He approached nearly soundlessly, rose up on his hind legs behind my assailant and sank huge, gleaming white teeth into the arm Kestor was using to restrain me.

Zach Kestor let out a yell that the city-citizens miles away in Peoria probably heard loud and clear, even over the howling wind. He went down on one knee, dragging me with him and trying to shake Rowdy loose, but Rowdy now not only looked a bit like a bear, he sounded a good deal like one, and even knowing Rowdy as I did, it was very intimidating. And while Kestor was otherwise occupied, I twisted away from him, stumbled forward, grabbed the brass statue and belted him with it.

It didn't knock him out, or anything remotely similar, but it did open a cut on his head that began to leak blood in copious amounts. He yelled again and tried to stand up, with Rowdy snarling and roaring and worrying at his arm. By then I had backed away from him and was gritting my teeth, which—had Kestor known me at all—might have made him wave the white flag. Duane would have recommended it. Instead, Kestor made one more attempt to rise. Dragging a 140 pound dog, that was no mean feat. Feeling Kestor's weight shift, Rowdy shook his head, his teeth still buried in the man's upper arm, and Kestor howled in pain.

"Stay down," I said coldly. "Stay down, or I swear I'll hit you again!" I held the statue over my shoulder and swung it slightly toward him, threatening. Fury was singing through my veins, and the pain in my shoulder felt distant and muted.

Kestor hesitated for a moment, his face a mask of pain and anger, but he stayed down. He slumped backward onto the floor with my dog's bared teeth an inch away from his face and blood pooling behind his head. I noticed with satisfaction several spots of Rowdy drool staining his shirt front.

"Get your dog off!" Kestor said weakly.

"Not a chance," I answered. "Stay down."

I edged away from Kestor and the suddenly-ferocious Rowdy, grabbed my cell phone and dialed 9-1-1.

Chapter Nineteen

I wasn't to know how lucky I had been until the knock on the door several days later. We got up from lunch and I went to answer, turning the knob against the newly-installed security latch. Brad Stanton stood on the doorstep, sharp and handsome in his uniform with his thick brown hair tossed in the brisk wind.

"Hello, Marianne." I released the latch and let him in. At Brad's use of my first name, Duffy looked from me to Brad. Brad looked from me to Duffy, and I looked from Duffy to Brad, pushing down a smile. Such encounters are the stuff of a French farce, but I liked both of these men very well, and I would have been distressed at any awkwardness. "Um," Brad said. "I wanted to bring you up to date on things since your assault."

"Would you like to sit down? Duffy, this is Officer Brad Stanton of the county sheriff's department.

Brad, please meet my good friend, Duffy Murray."
Brad edged toward a chair, and I urged him into it.

"How's your shoulder?" he asked.

"Doing great," I answered. "A few days without anyone yanking on it, and it was right as rain."

"That's good."

There was a short silence. Then, "Coffee, anyone?" I said brightly, and when Duffy and Brad both nodded, I escaped to the kitchen.

As the pot burped merrily away, I cleared away Duffy's and my lunch dishes and laid out my Blue Willow mugs. I could hear voices emanating from the living room, but I couldn't tell if they were friendly or frosty. Thus, when the coffee had finished brewing, and I poured out the rich black liquid, I re-entered the living room with a certain amount of trepidation. There I found Duffy enlightening Brad on the intricacies of playing Aces High No Trump Euchre, the two of them apparently thick as a couple of thieves.

"He's a Euchre aficionado. Knows all the variations!" Duffy exclaimed when I offered him his coffee. "We should have a foursome!"

"Great," I said mildly. "Brad, you have information to share about my little drama out here?"

Brad sipped his coffee. "Yes, I do. Here's what is probably the most important. Kestor had Kenny Probst doing his dirty work for him, hanging around your house and watching, and trying to get into the basement to retrieve the document. That's who Ashley saw." Brad took a sip of his coffee and went on. "Kenny's heart wasn't in it, though. I think the death of his brother really rattled him. I mentioned to you when we had lunch in Prairie City …" Brad hesitated, and I kept my gaze steadily on his face, though I knew Duffy's eyes had flicked to me. "… that we'd interviewed Kestor once on suspicion, but he was alibied for the time of the robbery, an alibi supplied by Kenny Probst, of course, or at least in part. He had some help with the cover-up, and we had no proof he was involved in the theft beyond our knowledge of the Probst brothers' and Kestor's association. Kenny has skipped town, by the way, which is probably why Zach Kestor landed on your doorstep. He finally had to take matters into his own hands. We'll catch up with Kenny. He was never the brains nor the brawn of their three-person club, and he'll give himself up eventually, if we don't find him. Kestor, on the other hand, is in a peck of trouble. Even without the robbery, which I feel sure we'll tie up, he entered your home, attacked you and was carrying a weapon."

"A weapon?" I gasped, and Duffy stood up abruptly, sloshing his coffee onto the carpet. He tossed a napkin over the spill and stepped on it, soaking up the liquid. "Sorry," he murmured.

I patted his arm. "I'll get it later." Duffy stayed standing. He set his cup down and paced from the picture window to the kitchen door and back again, running his fingers through his hair.

Brad watched him. "Kestor had a knife," he went on. "Sheathed, but on him. No telling whether he would have used it on you if your dog hadn't gotten to him first. Did he try to pull it?"

I thought back. "No, I don't think so."

I looked fondly at Rowdy, who was deeply asleep by the door to the porch. I wondered if he was drooling, but I didn't care. It gave me a chill to imagine what might have happened if Kestor had used his knife. Would my dog still be dozing peacefully, or would he be at the veterinarian's or worse? Would I be here having this conversation?

"You gave Kestor quite a wallop on the head," Brad said. "He had to have several stitches."

"Good," I answered unapologetically.

"If Kestor's such a pro, how come he came in the house with Rowdy here?" asked Duffy, stopping his pacing for a moment.

"I'm not sure," answered Brad. "My guess? He didn't know you had a dog. I have the feeling when we run Kenny to ground we'll find he isn't too happy with his buddy, Kestor. Kestor took off and left Marcus behind, don't forget, and now Marcus is dead. Maybe Kenny figured Kestor could discover the dog on his own."

Duffy nodded, staring out the window. "It seems like a pretty big risk to take, all for a piece of paper that no one has found."

Brad glanced at me. "Well, Kestor didn't know how much Marcus had told us before he was hit and killed. He might have thought we had more information than we actually did, or that he'd told us exactly where to find the document, and it was a matter of time before we came after him. Truthfully, most of what Marcus told us was pretty incoherent. He was mighty mad at Kestor, and he was cursing a blue streak, on top of running while on a cell phone. Not the best way to communicate."

"No," I said. "But it would be nice to have the paper. You said the one I thought it might be wasn't it." The sheriff had taken with them for evidence the bag of recycling from the basement and all the newspaper articles I had intended to give to the historical society, along with my improvised weapon.

"Well, about that." Brad looked down at his hands. "The statue? The one you clipped Zach Kestor with? Where did you get it?"

"I brought it up from the basement," I answered promptly. "It was one of the only things I kept from the great cleanout."

Brad smiled. "It seems it was keeping a little secret."

"What do you mean?" I exclaimed. "What secret?"

"When we got it back to the station we discovered a rolled up piece of paper hidden in the bottom. We took it out and—guess what?—Marcus Probst's fingerprints are all over it, and it's got the information he was yelling about when he called the station before he was killed."

I stared at Brad with my mouth open. "I hit Kestor over the head with the statue and the statue had inside it what he'd come looking for to start with?" I set my coffee cup on the end table and dropped back limply in my chair.

Duffy laughed and Brad shook his head. "It's poetic justice, right?"

"The statue was out in the piles in the yard," I protested. "We brought it up from the basement and left it there! Kenny Probst was trolling through the piles, and he didn't find it? This makes no sense!"

"You said you never saw him. Maybe he didn't go through the piles," Duffy reminded me.

"We'll know more when we find Kenny," said Brad. "He didn't know what he was looking for either, and there was a lot of stuff in the basement. I can attest to that!" He laughed and Duffy frowned, tossing a quick look in my direction. I shrugged. "My theory," Brad went on, "is that Kestor was pushing him to look for it, and he wasn't really trying."

"Ashley Midden scared him away twice that we know of, and those are only the times she saw him.

And if Ashley scared him, he must have been pretty easy to scare."

"Right." Brad tipped his mug up and drained the last of his coffee. "We'll want you to testify as to what happened when Kestor broke in, but I think we've got what we need. And you shouldn't have any more trouble. I don't expect Kenny Probst is likely to come back. Keep an eye out, though. The security on your door is a good addition."

"Thanks," I said, and thought back briefly to the Battle of the Security Latch—Natalie, Duffy and Louise versus Marianne. I preferred to continue to think of Burtonville as cozy and neighborly, but I finally gave in to pressure. And after all, I didn't have to use the latch all of the time.

"Thanks for the coffee." Brad shrugged on his coat and turned to Duffy. "You're on for Euchre."

"Okay, then," said Duffy. I stopped myself—well, mostly stopped myself—wondering who the fourth would be.

Later in the day, when the sun was nearly down, Duffy and I went down to the basement. We took the brightest lightbulb we could find and twisted it into the socket, turned on the switch and let the white glow illuminate every corner of the room, every crevice, every shadowed niche and darkened recess. I even set a camping lantern on the workbench and turned up the LED to its highest setting. Then, with the room radiating light, Duffy

169

and I stood in the center and gazed around us, into all the nooks and cracks—anywhere harmful intent might have crept and secreted itself. It was a fanciful notion, but I liked the idea of supplanting any negative energy left behind, now that the recent trouble was over. And it worked. Somehow the basement took on a new aspect after our little exercise was complete.

Finally, I retrieved the lantern, and paused to offer a silent apology to any basement-dwelling creature, four-, six- or eight-legged, who might have been alarmed by the unwelcome intrusion into its darkened home, then Duffy and I made our way upstairs.

"I better head back to Peoria." Duffy smiled. "Work calls and all that."

"Okay," I said. "And thanks."

"You're welcome," he answered, and brushed his hand lightly across my hair. "'Til we meet again."

"'Til then," I echoed. I watched until his car was out of sight, then went back in the house, blowing on my hands to warm them. Sighing, I flopped down on the couch and put out a hand to ruffle Rowdy's fur.

My tiny house on Beale Street wasn't whimsical or sassy yet—although it was getting there—but it was definitely beautiful, and it was all mine.

About the Author

Loraine J Hudson lives and writes in a small town in Michigan. She loves oldies rock music, stained glass, digging in her garden, playing with her dogs, horseback riding and, of course, writing. She is often at her most creative when she is taking her ex-racehorse out for an amble through the woods.

Using her pen name, Judith Wade, she has created a series of middle grades/YA chapter books that incorporate a little bit of fantasy and adventure.

Visit her at: http://facebook.com/authorlorainehudson and https://www.facebook.com/Author-Judith-Wade-1604938333105435/

Acknowledgements

Kudos to my beta readers!

Sarah Cushion

Judy Hudson

Sue Kaminga

Randy Pearson

...And a special thank you to David Ostrem, who was patient with my naïve questions about police procedure.

Made in the USA
Middletown, DE
02 May 2021